THE SWINDLER'S TREASURE

The Riverboat Adventures

1. *Escape Into the Night*
2. *Race for Freedom*
3. *Midnight Rescue*
4. *The Swindler's Treasure*

Adventures of the Northwoods

1. *The Disappearing Stranger*
2. *The Hidden Message*
3. *The Creeping Shadows*
4. *The Vanishing Footprints*
5. *Trouble at Wild River*
6. *The Mysterious Hideaway*
7. *Grandpa's Stolen Treasure*
8. *The Runaway Clown*
9. *Mystery of the Missing Map*
10. *Disaster on Windy Hill*

9610

THE RIVERBOAT ADVENTURES

The Swindler's Treasure

LOIS WALFRID JOHNSON

BETHANY HOUSE PUBLISHERS
MINNEAPOLIS, MINNESOTA 55438

The Swindler's Treasure

Frederick Douglass, John Jones, Samuel Morse, Priscilla Baltimore, Major Charles and Rebecca Hunter, John Livingston, Thomas Dimmock, Benjamin Godfrey, Dr. Thomas Brown, Frances Brown, J. W. Gilson, John Hart, Allan Pinkerton, William Florville, and Abraham Lincoln are historic characters who lived in the 1850s. Elijah Lovejoy died in 1837. All other characters are fictitious. Any resemblance to persons living or dead is coincidental.

Cover illustration by Angelo
Story illustrations by Catherine McLaughlin
Side-wheeler illustration by Toni Auble
Map of Upper Mississippi by Meridan Mapping
Sign language chart courtesy of the Illinois School for the Deaf, Jacksonville

Scripture quotations are from the King James Version of the Bible.

Published by Bethany House Publishers
A Ministry of Bethany Fellowship, Inc.
11300 Hampshire Avenue South
Minneapolis, Minnesota 55438

Printed in the United States of America.

Library of Congress Cataloging-in-Publication Data

Johnson, Lois Walfrid.
The swindler's treasure / by Lois Walfrid Johnson.
p. cm. — (The riverboat adventures ; #4)
Summary: In 1857, while working for the Underground Railroad on a Mississippi River steamboat, thirteen-year-old Libby hunts for the swindler who has robbed her father, and she tries to reunite the fugitive slave Jordan with his missing father.
ISBN 1–55661–354–7
[1. Underground railroad—Fiction. 2. Fugitive slaves—Fiction. 3. Slavery—Fiction. 4. Afro-Americans—Fiction. 5. Steamboats—Fiction. 6. Mississippi River—Fiction. 7. Christian life—Fiction.] I. Title. II. Series: Johnson, Lois Walfrid. Riverboat adventures ; #4
PZ7.J63255Sw 1997
[Fic]—dc21 97–4670
CIP
AC

To the people of Alton, Illinois,
and the surrounding area
who have believed in the worth
and freedom of all people;

and

to Kathleen Cook and Marene Mattern
and
every student at the Illinois School for the Deaf:
You showed me your hands
to help me hear.

LOIS WALFRID JOHNSON is the bestselling author of twenty-seven books. Her work has been translated into twelve languages and has received many awards, including the Gold Medallion, the C. S. Lewis Silver Medal, the Wisconsin State Historical Society Award, and five Silver Angels from Excellence in Media. Yet Lois believes that one of her greatest rewards is knowing that readers enjoy her books.

In her fun times Lois likes to camp, bike, cross-country ski, be with family and friends, and talk with young people like you. Lois and her husband, Roy, live in Minnesota.

In the time in which this book is set,
African Americans were called *Negro,*
the Spanish word for black,
or *colored people.*

Contents

1. The Swindler's Threat 13
2. Disaster! 19
3. Run! 27
4. Strange Reunion 33
5. Peter James Christopherson 42
6. The Big Search 50
7. Happy Birthday! 61
8. Jordan's Daddy 70
9. Secret in the Rock 80
10. The Deserted House 89
11. Caleb's Hero 99
12. Narrow Escape 106
13. Last Chance? 115
14. The Heat of the Furnace 123
15. The Disappearing Package 134
16. Big Bullies 142
17. Fire! 151
18. Mr. Lincoln's Springfield 161
19. Trick Or...? 171
20. Nobody Knows 178

Sign Language: How to Finger Spell the Alphabet 187
Acknowledgments 188

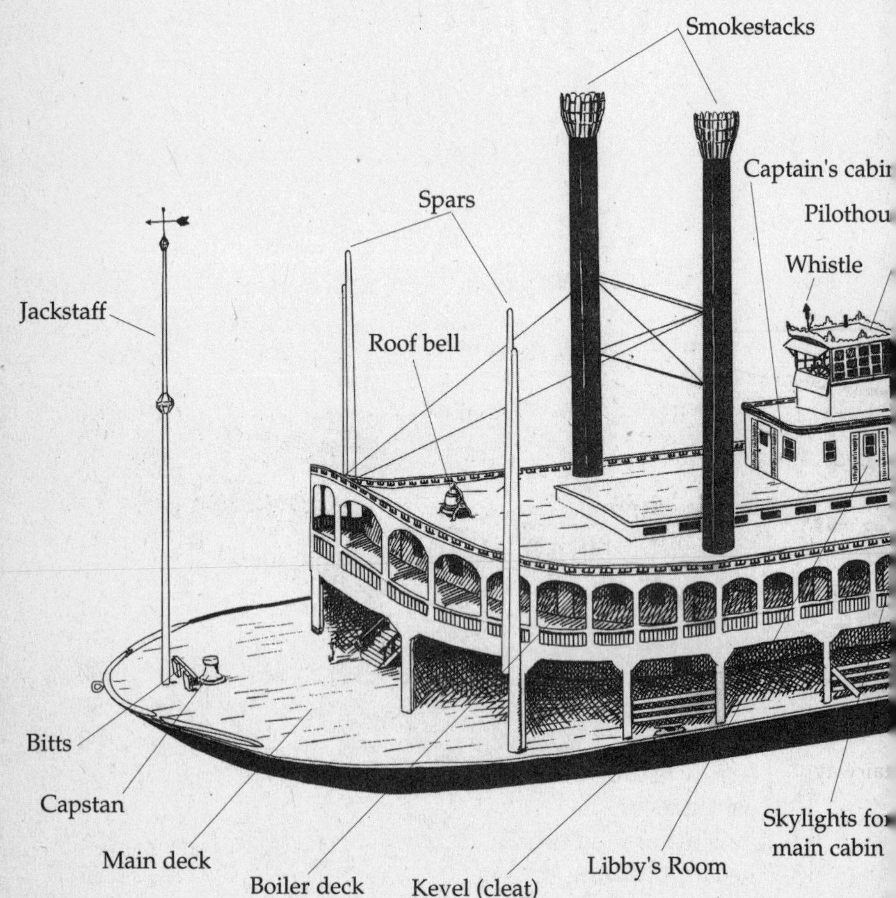
Smokestacks
Captain's cabi
Pilothou
Whistle
Spars
Jackstaff
Roof bell
Bitts
Capstan
Main deck
Boiler deck
Kevel (cleat)
Libby's Room
Skylights fo
main cabin

The Side-Wheeler Christina

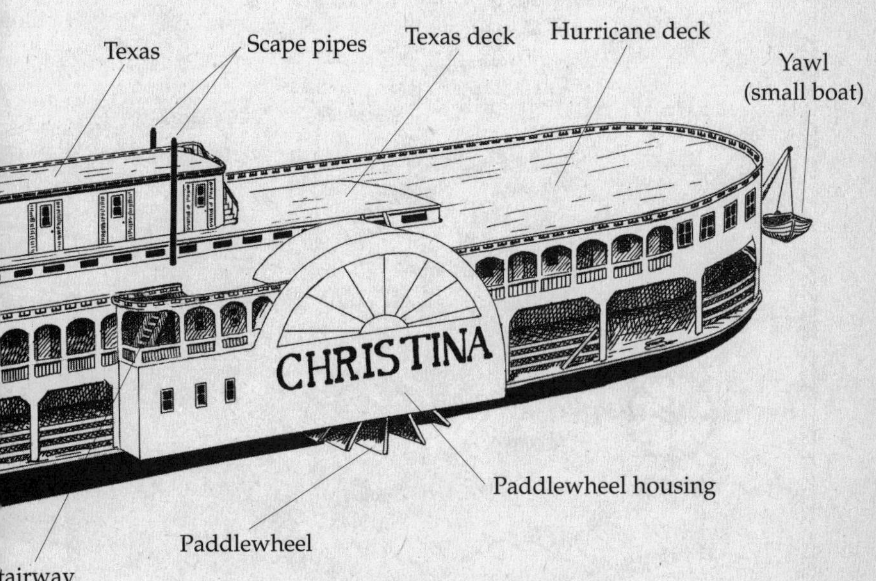

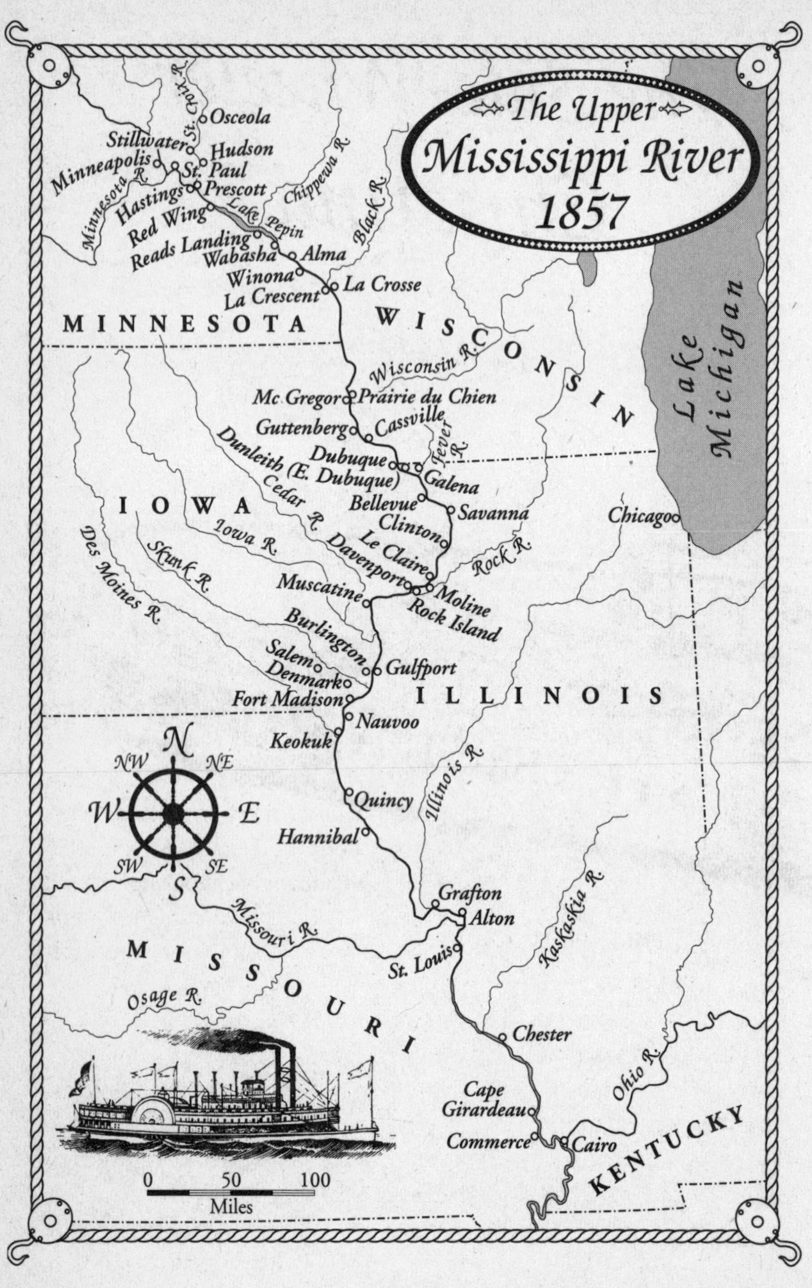
The Upper
Mississippi River
1857
MINNESOTA
WISCONSIN
IOWA
ILLINOIS
MISSOURI
KENTUCKY
Lake Michigan
Osceola
Stillwater
Hudson
Minneapolis
St. Paul
Hastings
Prescott
Red Wing
Reads Landing
Wabasha
Alma
Winona
La Crescent
La Crosse
Lake Pepin
St. Croix R.
Minnesota R.
Chippewa R.
Black R.
Wisconsin R.
Mc Gregor
Prairie du Chien
Guttenberg
Cassville
Fever R.
Dubuque
Dunleith (E. Dubuque)
Galena
Bellevue
Savanna
Clinton
Chicago
Le Claire
Cedar R.
Iowa R.
Skunk R.
Des Moines R.
Rock R.
Davenport
Moline
Rock Island
Muscatine
Burlington
Salem
Denmark
Gulfport
Fort Madison
Nauvoo
Keokuk
Quincy
Hannibal
Illinois R.
Grafton
Alton
St. Louis
Missouri R.
Osage R.
Kaskaskia R.
Chester
Cape Girardeau
Commerce
Cairo
Ohio R.
N
NW
NE
W
E
SW
SE
S
0
50
100
Miles

1

The Swindler's Threat

A sharp wind rattled the windows, sounding just as angry as the voices. Libby Norstad's deep brown eyes held a question: *What's wrong?*

The sound came from somewhere outside the *Christina*'s dining room. Pushing back her deep red hair, Libby listened. *Men's voices*, she decided. *Among them, Pa's.*

As she hurried out to the wide stairway at the front of the steamboat, the voices grew louder. At the bottom of the steps, Libby's father, the captain of the *Christina*, stood on the main deck. With him were two men.

"But Mr. Dexter is helping me," one of them said. From his accent Libby knew he was an immigrant.

The other man was well dressed, red-faced, and angry looking. Pa turned to him.

"Mr. Dexter?" The captain's quiet voice held a ring of steel that told Libby he was angry too. "Mr. Edward Dexter?"

Already a crowd had gathered around to listen. Feeling concerned for Pa, twelve-year-old Libby sat down on the steps to watch.

"Your reputation has gone ahead of you, Mr. Dexter," Captain Norstad said. "Up and down the Mississippi River, respectable captains have told you to get off their boat. And I'm telling you now!"

"No! No!" the immigrant cried. "Look what Mr. Dexter is doing for me!" As though unable to believe his good luck, he held up a well-stuffed sack.

"Mr. Iverson, when did you buy your land?" Captain Norstad asked.

The immigrant's face shone with pride. "For one year I have worked. I have cleared a field. I have planted corn. I have built a house—and a barn for my cow."

Digging into the sack, Mr. Iverson held up a fistful of paper money. "Now I will buy more land."

Captain Norstad took one bill, then two, then five or six. Turning them toward the light, he studied the bills carefully. "You are selling the farm you have?" he asked.

"If a man is willing to work, the streets of America are paved with gold! I will take this money and buy a bigger farm."

The captain's "No!" sounded like an explosion. "Look at this!" He held a dollar bill close to the immigrant's face. "Look at the name of the bank on this greenback! This is wildcat money!"

"Wildcat?" Mr. Iverson peered at the bill. "We have no wildcats on my farm."

"It's called wildcat money because it comes from a bad bank!"

Captain Norstad turned to Mr. Dexter. "You are offering him money printed by a bank with a reputation as awful as your own."

"No! No!" the immigrant exclaimed again. "Mr. Dexter is giving me twice as much money as I paid for my farm. A good return on my hard work, yah?"

"It is not a good return," the captain answered. "He is giving you money that is worth nothing!"

"You mean counterfeit?"

"Just about," the captain said. "The United States government doesn't print money now. It gives permission to state banks to print the money."

"So!" Mr. Iverson declared. "American money is good money."

"Sometimes good. Sometimes bad."

"Bad? If America says print the money, why bad?"

Captain Norstad sighed. "I wish I knew your language so I could explain better. If you take this money to a bank and say, 'I want to buy a new farm,' they would look at you and say, 'These paper bills are not worth a cent. The bank that printed this money has no gold in it.' "

"Yah?" Mr. Iverson looked even more confused. "I don't understand what you say."

"It's simple." Captain Norstad spoke slowly. "Edward Dexter is a swindler."

"Ha!" Dexter scoffed. "The captain wants to keep you from getting rich. This is between you and me."

With troubled eyes Mr. Iverson looked from one man to the other. In that third week of May 1857, countless immigrants were traveling to their new homes in America. Often they found it hard to know whom they should trust.

Captain Norstad paid no attention to Dexter. "Do you have a wife?" the captain asked Mr. Iverson.

The immigrant nodded. "I go to meet her now. She is coming on train from the Old Country."

"Do you have children?"

"One girl and two boys. They will be proud of what their papa has done in America."

"No!" Captain Norstad shook his head. "They will think, 'An evil man made a fool of my papa.' Do you want your wife and your children to have no house?"

"No house?" Fear filled Mr. Iverson's eyes. "I have worked hard to make a home in America."

Captain Norstad pointed to Edward Dexter. "This man will rob you of your home."

"Yah?" Still Mr. Iverson looked uncertain. "You are telling me the truth?" Again the immigrant looked from one man to the other. "Who should I believe?"

"The captain doesn't want you to make a lot of money," Dexter said quickly.

"Yah, it is a lot of money," the immigrant answered. "I can do many things for my family with this much money." He stretched out his hand toward the swindler. "We shake on it."

But Captain Norstad stepped between the two men. "No, you won't. I will not let you shake on it."

At the top of Mr. Iverson's open trunk lay a large Bible. The captain pointed to it. "You believe the words of this book?"

"Yah, it is truth."

"If I put my hand on your Bible and say, 'This man is a swindler,' would you believe me?"

"You would make your words so strong?"

"May I?" Captain Norstad asked.

Mr. Iverson nodded. As if expecting Captain Norstad to be struck dead, the farmer stepped back.

With a careful touch Captain Norstad reached down. As his hand rested on the Bible, his face showed how much the book meant to him. "I am telling you the truth," he said. "This man will cheat you of your land. His money is worthless."

"He is trying to make a fool of me?" the immigrant asked. "To take what I have?"

The captain nodded.

Still looking into Captain Norstad's eyes, Mr. Iverson reached down. With one quick movement, he put his hand over the captain's hand as it rested on the Bible. "I believe you." Without another word Mr. Iverson held out the bag filled with wildcat money.

His eyes blazing with anger, Edward Dexter snatched the bag. Holding up his clenched fist, he shook it at the captain. "If it's the last thing I do, I'll get even with you!"

Libby felt a chill down her spine. No doubt about it: Edward Dexter was a dangerous man. But her father acted as if he hadn't heard the swindler's threat.

"Pack your bags!" the captain said to Dexter. "In twenty minutes we'll reach Fairport, Iowa. You're getting off there."

"You can't do this to me!"

"I already have. Be here on the deck or I'll send my crew after you. I'll stand at the gangplank till you get off this boat."

As though wondering if anyone would help him fight the captain, the swindler looked around. At the edge of the crowd stood Jordan Parker, a runaway slave who worked for Captain Norstad. For a moment the swindler's gaze rested on Jordan, as though memorizing every detail of his appearance.

Quietly Jordan edged back into the crowd, but Libby knew it was too late. *Dexter will remember*, she thought, the fear within her growing. *If he guessed that Jordan is a fugitive, Dexter will know there is a big reward on his head.*

Through fugitive slave laws, Congress had strengthened the right of slave owners to hunt down and capture fugitives, even in free northern states. Owners often hired slave catchers—rough, cruel men—to bring back runaways.

In that moment Libby remembered Jordan's family. If Dexter somehow discovered they were hiding on the boat, Pa could go to prison, or lose the *Christina*, or both.

Libby shivered. *Will Edward Dexter try to get money any way he can? Pa seems to think so.*

When the swindler stalked away, the crowd broke up. Libby ran down the steps to her father. Moving over to one side of the deck, Pa stood where he and Libby could talk without other people listening.

The knot of dread in Libby's stomach was growing. "What if Dexter finds a way to get even? He knows that the *Christina* stops at every town on the Mississippi River."

Pa sighed. "As captain, I could have arrested Dexter if he passed counterfeit money. But he did something legal, even though it's wrong."

As the *Christina* steamed toward the next town, Libby kept thinking about the swindler's clenched fist. "Dexter can wait for us. He knows where you'll be before you get there."

"Sometimes there's a cost to doing the right thing," Pa said.

"And a reward?" Libby didn't want to think about what might lie ahead.

"The reward of knowing you've done what's right. I run a family boat. I can't let someone do whatever he wants."

A strong light glowed in her father's eyes. Looking at him, Libby felt proud of the kind of person he was. Yet, like a warning deep inside, Libby also felt uneasy about the swindler's threat.

While the *Christina* tied up at Fairport, Captain Norstad watched the stairs. Suddenly he spoke to Libby. "Quick! Move away so Dexter doesn't know you're my daughter."

As Libby joined the passengers waiting to leave, the swindler reached the bottom of the stairs. In each hand he held a carpet-bag—a cloth bag with two handles. Acting as though he owned the boat, Edward Dexter walked around the people waiting in line.

When he reached the captain, the swindler tipped his hat and strolled down the gangplank.

Strange, Libby thought. *Dexter doesn't look angry.*

Pa looked as puzzled as Libby felt. As the swindler hurried away, Pa stared after him.

A short distance from the river, Dexter turned around to face the *Christina.* For a moment he stood there, as if studying every line of the beautiful white steamboat. Like a cat licking his whiskers, the swindler seemed pleased with himself.

As though it were still happening, Libby remembered the man shaking his clenched fist at Pa. Now the expression on Dexter's face frightened Libby even more.

2

Disaster!

"Captain Norstad." Caleb Whitney stood next to Libby's pa and spoke in a low voice. "We're ready for you."

The darkness of night surrounded them, but Caleb's blond hair looked as windswept as the day had been. Slender and strong, he had lived on the *Christina* since his grandmother became head pastry cook. Now Caleb's blue eyes held a look that told Libby something important was about to happen.

Pa's cabin boy, she thought. *The person who is supposed to run Pa's errands, see that his clothes are pressed, polish his shoes*. Yet Caleb did much more than that.

In March when Libby came to live on the *Christina*, the thirteen-year-old boy had seemed a mystery to her. Then she discovered who Caleb really was. As a conductor in the Underground Railroad, he helped runaway slaves travel from one hiding place to the next. Since the age of nine, Caleb had worked for Pa in the secret plan that helped fugitives reach freedom.

The night before, Jordan's mother, brother, and two sisters had slipped on board at Burlington, Iowa. Except for Jordan, who also worked as a cabin boy, Libby hadn't seen any of the family since. After continuing upriver, the *Christina* had made several long stops to unload and take on freight.

Now, with the moon high in the sky, the deck passengers had made their beds wherever they could find space on the main deck. Peace and quiet had settled over the boat. Caleb had picked his moment, and it was right.

With growing curiosity Libby followed him and Pa. Without making a sound, Caleb led them past the wide stairway at the front of the *Christina*. After a quick look around, he opened the door into the cargo space.

The large open room was filled with freight. Caleb closed the door behind Libby, then stood just inside, waiting and watching. As Libby peered into the darkness, Caleb lit a lantern and led them deeper into the room.

All around them boxes and barrels were piled high, making weird shapes in the half-light. To Libby's surprise Caleb passed the entrance to the secret hiding place. Then he turned sideways and slipped through a narrow opening between tall piles of freight. When Pa, then Libby, followed, she discovered a hidden-away space, like a small room without a ceiling.

Here, where there was more room than in the secret hiding place, Caleb set the lantern on the floor. Its flame lit the faces of the people who waited but left everything else in darkness.

Jordan Parker, the runaway slave, sat cross-legged with his little sister Rose in his lap. On either side of Jordan were his eight-year-old brother, Zack, and his eleven-year-old sister, Serena. As Pa and Caleb sat down, Libby found a place next to Serena, and the small circle was complete.

"Welcome aboard, Hattie," Pa said as if he hadn't been able to talk with Jordan's mother before. "Your son Jordan is a fine young man."

With her gaze on the floor, the way she had been taught by her former masters, Hattie nodded her thanks.

Jordan had led his family on the dangerous trip out of slavery. Usually Caleb moved runaways on as soon as it was safe. Because Jordan worked for him, the captain cared even more than usual about what happened to the family.

"We're close to a good place to let you off," Captain Norstad said. "The Underground Railroad will help you across Illinois and Lake Michigan to Canada."

Jordan's mother shook her head. "We ain't ready to go to Canada." For a moment she looked at her children. "We wants to find my husband—their daddy." Micah Parker had been sold away from the rest of the family, and none of them knew where he was.

"Where do you want to live while you're looking for him?" the captain asked Hattie. "Chicago? There's a large group of free blacks who would protect you. White people, too, who would help, and a detective named Allan Pinkerton."

But Jordan answered for his mother. "Chicago be all the way across Illinois. We need to be where we can get word about my daddy."

"We wants to live where people is moving around," Hattie added. Though she looked at the floorboards instead of the captain, her voice was strong and sure, as if she had often thought about the problem.

Watching her, Libby realized how much Jordan was like his mother. Both were tall and slender, but the likeness was more than that. Both of them knew what they wanted in life. While still a young boy, Jordan had begun to dream about bringing his family out of slavery.

"I is goin' to git a job and keep my head down," Hattie said now. "But when my head be down, I is goin' to ask questions till I find my husband."

"News goes up and down the river on boats," Jordan said. "We wants to be close to the river."

"But far enough away to be safe," Captain Norstad answered. For a minute he was silent, as though thinking about every town up and down the Mississippi River. One by one he seemed to check them off in his mind. Finally he said, "Galena, Illinois."

"Galena?" Hattie asked.

"In northwestern Illinois," the captain said. "It's only three or four miles up the Galena River, and the most important stop between St. Louis and St. Paul. There's a group of free blacks there, and people coming and going—people you can ask about your husband."

"Will my children be safe there?" In the flickering light Hattie looked at each one.

"I wish I could tell you they will be," the captain said. "But they'll be truly safe only in Canada. You understand about the fugitive slave laws?"

Hattie nodded. "Even in free states, I ain't got no rights. Slave catchers can snatch my children away from me."

Hattie's gaze rested on her oldest son. During the past year, Jordan had been sold to a cruel master named Riggs. From this new owner, Jordan had made a life-or-death escape.

"I keep thinkin' about Jordan," Hattie went on. "That master of his said no slave ever got away from him alive."

Libby looked across the circle to Caleb. More than once they had talked about whether Riggs would make a special effort to capture Jordan for that very reason. Libby waited for Pa's answer.

"Riggs is a busy man—a rich man with many interests," he said. "I hope that he doesn't have time to chase around after one runaway. I hope he's forgotten Jordan by now."

But it's only two months since he escaped, Libby thought. Again she glanced at Caleb. This time their gaze met, as if he, too, wondered how long Riggs would remember. Not only had Riggs been Jordan's owner, but a cruel slavetrader as well.

"Wherever you live, Jordan needs to be careful," Captain Norstad told Hattie. "I have friends in Galena, and I could help you find work. But I wish you'd think about a place farther away from where you were a slave—a place where life would be easier for you."

Once more looking at the floorboards, Hattie spoke softly. "Life ain't easy, Captain Norstad. It ain't easy for you or for me. You has made some hard choices, and my family be one of them."

The light of the lantern showed the strength in Hattie's face. "I thanks you for all you has done. For helpin' Jordan. For hidin' us. For helpin' me find work when I gits off the boat. But, Captain Norstad—"

For the first time Hattie looked up. Wearing the proud look Libby had often seen in Jordan, Hattie sat tall and straight. "How can I be happy being free if my husband ain't?"

A smile flashed across the captain's face. "I suspect you're right, Hattie. When we reach Galena, I'll let you off there."

Inwardly Libby groaned. *I won't get to know Serena.* She would leave the boat before they even had a chance to talk.

When Pa stood up to leave, Libby wanted to take her time and talk to Serena. Yet Libby knew she had to be careful. The longer all of them stayed together, the bigger the risk that the wrong person would find them. Knowing that she had no choice but to follow Pa, Libby spoke softly.

"Good-bye, Serena. I hope I see you again." Libby saw the glad light in Serena's face.

"Good-bye, Miss Libby," she said, her voice shy but clear.

Then Caleb picked up the lantern. Libby followed him and Pa through the darkness back through the cargo area to the front of the boat. There Caleb slipped away, and Pa and Libby started up the stairway to their rooms.

On the next deck up, a frightened-looking young man spoke to them. "I need to talk to you, Captain."

Captain Norstad took one look at the mud clerk and said, "Let's go to the office."

Called the mud clerk because he often stood in the mud while collecting fares, the young man had not worked long for Pa. In the office he dropped into a chair as if no longer able to stand. Libby and Pa joined him at the table.

In the lamplight the clerk's face looked pale. "I have bad news," he began.

"What is it?" the captain asked as though anxious to get it over with.

The young man hesitated, as if dreading what he needed to say. "All the money you took in—" The clerk stopped as though afraid to go on.

"Yes?"

"The money we collected for freight—the money we got from passengers up and down the river—"

"Where is it?" the captain asked as if knowing where this was going to end.

The clerk's face was gray now. "I don't know."

"You don't *know*? I need that money for paying my crew. I need it for making payments on this boat."

"Yes, sir."

"If the money isn't here, what happened to it?" the captain asked. "The good money, I mean, that our senior clerk was so careful to take in?"

More than once Libby had seen the senior clerk check a book whenever there was a question about what was good money and what came from a wildcat bank. He had worked for Pa a long time and knew more than anyone about what bills were safe to accept.

"I put the money in the safe." The mud clerk stumbled on his words.

"And you closed the door?"

"I started to close the door." The clerk's face had changed again—pink now with embarrassment.

"You didn't lock the safe?" Captain Norstad's voice again held the steel that Libby knew was anger kept under control.

"No, sir."

"Let me guess," the captain answered. "A well-dressed man spoke to you, calling you away for some fool reason. You followed him. He gave you the slip. When you returned to the office, the safe was closed, even locked."

The clerk nodded.

"You thought, 'Hmmm. I locked the safe, after all.' When you opened the door, it was full of money. But just a minute ago, you took a better look."

When the clerk opened the safe, Libby saw two piles of bills. No doubt the small one was the money taken in since the swindler left the boat. With trembling hands the clerk lifted out the large pile of paper currency and set the bills in front of the captain.

Libby leaned forward to look. When she saw the name of the bank, tears welled up in her eyes. Even she knew that the money was worthless.

"Oh, Pa!" she wailed.

"Every bill?" the captain roared. "Every single bill is from this worthless bank?"

Twice the clerk tried to speak. When no sound came, he nodded.

"Do you know how much money was taken?" Pa asked.

The clerk knew. Moments before it was stolen, he had finished counting it.

"That is the money I cleared from all my trips since the opening of the season," Captain Norstad said as though trying to explain to a young child. "With it I planned to pay my crew and

make a big payment on the *Christina*. Do you understand what you have done?"

"No, sir," the clerk said. "I mean, yes, sir."

"When we reach Galena, I want you to get off," the captain said, his voice stiff with anger. "I want you to find a job where you learn to handle responsibility. Until then don't let me see your face."

Without another word the clerk crept out of the office. The moment he left, Pa kicked the door shut behind him. Elbows on the table, he closed his eyes and covered them with his hands.

Watching Pa, Libby felt even more afraid. Like water coming to a boil, her resentment changed into anger. Because of one man's carelessness and another man's theft, Pa's whole life had changed for the worse.

"The swindler got even," she said finally.

Without looking up, Pa nodded, as though unable to speak.

3

Run!

Then Pa reached out and pulled Libby close in a hug. "It's the people who work for me I'm most concerned about. People like Caleb's grandmother. My whole crew. How am I going to pay all of them?"

Libby felt as if a lump had formed in her throat. "If the swindler makes you lose the *Christina,* he'll be taking our home. He'll be taking the way you earn our living." Libby lowered her voice. "And you won't have a way to help runaway slaves."

"That's what would bother me the most." Pa shook his head, as though still not believing what had happened. "When Dexter tried to swindle the immigrant, I couldn't arrest him. Now I could arrest him for being a thief. But I don't know where he is."

During the four long years after her mother's death, Libby had lived with her aunt in Chicago. Libby always felt glad she could be with Pa again. "I thought the *Christina* was paid for," she said in a small voice.

"It was," her father answered. "Last fall, before you came to live with me, we had a lot of ice damage. I needed to have the entire hull rebuilt. When we get to Galena, I'll talk to the man who loaned me the money."

Galena. The city in northwestern Illinois that was settled early because of lead mines in the area. The town had become a legend because of the lead shipped from there to St. Louis. Some riverboat captains had made their fortunes in the trade. But now, because of the swindler, Pa faced enormous debt.

What if he loses everything he's worked for? Libby couldn't imagine such a life. Even more, she couldn't imagine Pa not being able to do what he believed in—helping fugitive slaves.

Early the next morning, the *Christina* entered the Galena River. Here and there clumps of birches grew along the banks. Willow branches hung low, and Libby caught the scent of wet earth and new growth. Before long the steamboat reached the city of Galena. Throwing out the lines, or ropes, deckhands tied up between two other paddle-wheelers.

Though he was usually tall and strong looking, Pa's shoulders slumped with discouragement as he walked down the gangplank.

An hour later he was back. "Tell Jordan I have a place for his family," Pa said to Caleb. "Tell them to leave now, a few at a time, while we're unloading freight. The market is busy, and they can find each other there. After they walk around awhile, they should follow you at a distance to the right house."

"C'mon, Libby," Caleb said when Pa finished giving directions. "Let's go talk to Jordan."

They found him in the cargo area. When Caleb told the good news, an excited light shone in Jordan's eyes. Then Caleb clapped Jordan on the back. Watching Caleb, Libby knew it was hard for him to say good-bye. The two boys had become good friends, in the way Libby had hoped she could get to know Serena.

But Jordan had one more question. "Do you know how I can find my daddy?"

Caleb glanced over his shoulder, then lowered his voice. "Libby's pa said there's a way. But it's dangerous."

"Can I do it?" Jordan asked.

Caleb shrugged. "Captain Norstad didn't tell me. I just know there's a big risk. He wants us to ask around first. One of us might hear something."

Leaving Jordan in the cargo area, Libby and Caleb found a place to sit near the bow of the *Christina*. From there they watched Jordan's family begin their new life.

His mother, Hattie, went first, carrying little Rose. A few minutes later, Serena and Zack slipped down the gangplank. Jordan was the last to go. He glanced toward Caleb and Libby with one quick grin. It was easy to see Jordan's excitement about what was ahead.

"Will he be safe?" Libby asked Caleb.

"I hope so." Caleb waited till his friend disappeared in the crowded marketplace. Then he, too, left the *Christina*.

Not until Caleb returned and the steamboat headed back down the Galena River did Libby get a chance to talk to Pa. Standing next to the railing on the second deck up, he told her what happened.

"The man who holds the loan was good to me," Pa said. "Up till now I've paid on time. He said I could make a double payment on August fifteenth."

"Three months from now." Libby felt relieved. On that May evening, August fifteenth seemed a long time away.

But Pa wasn't finished. "If I can't make the double payment, I won't get another chance. I'll lose the boat."

"Lose the *Christina*?" To Libby it was unthinkable. "You named the boat for Ma!"

Reaching out, Libby ran her hand along the smooth railing. She had always believed the *Christina* was the most beautiful steamboat on the river.

"After all your hard work?" she asked. "It's not fair!"

Pa smiled. "Sometimes life isn't fair, Libby. That's not what counts. I'll pray and work my hardest so we don't lose the *Christina*. But even if we do, the Lord will be with us."

"Even if we do?" Libby swallowed hard, just thinking about it. *Even if the Lord is with us, I can't think of anything worse than losing the* Christina. But she didn't dare say that to Pa.

"Wherever we go, we'll look for the swindler," her father promised. "Maybe we'll find both him and the money he stole."

Libby pushed her frightened thoughts away. "If you have a good season—"

"And the Lord's protection," Pa said. "Let's pray for both."

But Libby knew all the dangerous things that happened to steamboats. They exploded or caught fire or struck the hidden roots of old trees and sank within minutes.

Finding the treasure of all that saved-up money? Even the idea seemed impossible.

On the way back down the Mississippi River, Pa stopped at Fairport, the town where he had let Edward Dexter off. No one remembered seeing a man of his description. The swindler had probably taken the next steamboat that came along.

At several other places, Pa asked about him. Somehow Edward Dexter had vanished into thin air. That bothered Libby even more.

During the months of June and July, Libby and Caleb talked often about Jordan's family. To their great disappointment, the *Christina* did not visit Galena even once. Pa had gotten several good jobs hauling freight close to St. Louis instead.

Always Libby watched the money that was taken in. By the end of June, Pa was able to pay the money he owed the crew. In July he started building up the profit needed to make one payment. But a double payment? Libby was afraid to ask about it. She only knew her father was losing weight from working so hard.

August fifteenth, Libby thought more than once. Often she counted the days. Without doubt she knew Pa didn't have the money he needed.

Then, less than a month before the loan was due, Pa told Libby they were going back to Galena. Early Saturday morning, on the fourth weekend in July, they again steamed up the Galena

River. Libby and Caleb sat high on the hurricane deck to watch all that was going on. From the steamboat ahead of them came the slap of great paddle wheels against the water.

"How do you think Serena is doing?" The morning sunlight touched Libby's deep red hair, bringing out the gold. "Remember how excited Jordan looked the last time we saw him?"

Both Libby and Caleb could hardly wait to see Jordan and his family. But now Caleb said, "I hope we find Jordan in Galena."

It had never occurred to Libby that he might not be there. "Where would he go?"

Caleb shrugged, but he looked uneasy.

"Jordan's smart," Libby said. "He wouldn't go off without a good reason."

"He's got the biggest reason of all—finding his father."

When Caleb grew quiet, Libby's thoughts tumbled on. "His father. If someone told Jordan he knew something about his father. Where he is, for instance—" Libby hated to even say what she was thinking. "Remember? We talked about it."

Caleb remembered, all right. "The one time when Jordan doesn't use good judgment is when he gets scared about his family."

When the *Christina* tied up at the busy mining city, the waterfront swarmed with activity. Caleb, Libby, and her dog, Samson, stood on the main deck, watching the steamboats around them. The great black Newfoundland had been a present from Pa when Libby came to live on board. As though eager for a good run, Samson kept edging toward the gangplank.

The moment he touched land, the dog raced off. Picking up a stick in his mouth, he brought it to where Libby stood on the riverbank. Each time she threw it out, he tore after it.

"Let's hunt up Jordan," Caleb said as Samson brought back the stick. But someone called to Caleb.

"Go ahead and look around the market," he told Libby. "I'll catch up."

A few blocks away from the river, Libby came to the marketplace. Farmers from the surrounding area stood alongside their wagons, selling whatever produce they had and swapping stories. For a time Libby looked at their horses—large draft animals with great hooves and strong bodies.

Then Samson became restless. Instead of staying beside Libby, he kept roaming, sniffing his way into anything he could find. Libby decided to start walking.

Standing at the edge of Commerce Street, she waited while two wagons rumbled past. Across the street a blond boy hurried up a side street leading to the main part of town. Thinking it was Caleb, Libby started after him.

Just then she heard the clip-clop of a swiftly moving horse. Edging back from the street, Libby turned to see a buggy coming from her left. As she watched, the young driver lifted a whip. When it snaked out above his horse, the buggy picked up even more speed.

Close to Libby, the driver seemed to change his mind. At his signal the horse started to turn left. The buggy wobbled, then swayed as if it would tip.

Seeing the danger, Libby called out, "Caleb! Behind you!"

In that instant Samson broke away from Libby, racing ahead. Without looking around, the boy still hurried along the side of the street.

The next moment the buggy made the turn. Swinging wide, the horse headed straight toward Caleb.

"Hey!" the driver shouted. "Get out of my way!" But the blond boy did not look back.

Again the young man shouted. "What's the matter with you? Get out of my way!"

Closer and closer rolled the swiftly moving buggy. "Run, Caleb!" Libby screamed. "Run!"

4

Strange Reunion

His legs flying, Samson streaked along the street. Reaching the boy, the dog pushed him out of the way. Seconds later the horse and buggy clattered past.

When Libby caught up to her dog, the boy still lay on the ground. As he started to sit up, Libby got a better look at him. Now that she was closer, Libby saw that he was shorter than Caleb and thinner, too—maybe nine or ten years old at the most. Yet with his blond hair he could be Caleb's younger brother.

Looking after the buggy, the boy moved his hands and fingers, gesturing wildly.

Her heart still pounding, Libby dropped down on her knees. "Why didn't you get out of the way?"

Instead of answering, the boy stared up at her. Thinking that she was making him even more afraid, Libby tried to calm herself. "I'm glad you're okay," she said.

Like Caleb's, the boy's eyes were blue, but now they seemed filled with questions, or fear, or both.

"What's your name?" Libby asked.

But the boy threw his arms around Samson. "Thank you,

thank you," he mumbled into the dog's ear.

When the boy stumbled to his feet, Libby wanted to comfort him. "It wasn't your fault, but you need to walk facing the traffic so you can see if someone comes too fast. You need to listen."

Still petting the dog, the boy kept talking to Samson. When the dog licked the boy's hand, Libby saw the ragged edge of his blue shirt. Both of his pant legs had holes at the knees. Watching the boy, Libby wondered what to do. He didn't seem hurt, but why didn't he answer her?

Then from the street ahead of her, Libby heard Caleb calling. Still wondering if she was doing the right thing, Libby started out. When her dog didn't follow, she called to him. "C'mon, Samson!"

The dog started after her but kept turning back. Finally the boy waved to him as though saying good-bye, and the dog seemed more ready to follow Libby.

"What happened?" Caleb asked when Libby reached him. He had taken a different side street from the river.

Libby still felt shaky from the close call. As she told Caleb about it, she again looked around. The blond boy stood by the side of the street, watching them.

"He's okay?" Caleb asked.

"He seems to be," Libby said. "But I couldn't get him to talk to me. Samson pushed him out of the way just in time."

"We should find his parents," Caleb said. But when he and Libby started back, the boy ran in the opposite direction and disappeared between buildings.

Caleb stopped. "For some reason he seems afraid of us—like he doesn't trust us."

Libby agreed. That seemed the best description of the whole strange thing.

Deciding they should go on, Libby and Caleb turned onto Main Street. New brick buildings stood tall and beautiful along the winding road. On one side of the street, a high bluff rose directly behind the business places.

Caleb led Libby to a steep stairway. By the time they came

out a block higher, Libby was panting from all the steps. Above them, still higher up, large homes with tall board fences clung to the side of the bluff.

"You're sure you know where to go?" Libby asked.

"Yup. Jordan's mother works for a man who was a steamboat captain. When he fell on hard times, his wife turned their mansion into a boardinghouse."

When they came to the mansion, Caleb went around to the back. The person who answered the door sent them to the carriage house. In the lower half of the building, horses and buggies were kept.

Caleb led Libby up the flight of steps on the outside of the building. At the top of the stairs was a landing. There Caleb knocked on the door.

Serena opened it. When she saw them there, a smile spread across her face, reaching her dimples. To Libby's surprise she looked them straight in the eyes instead of keeping her gaze down.

"You wish to see Jordan?" Serena asked as if she had been trained to answer the door.

When Caleb nodded, Libby spoke quickly. "And we want to see *you*."

Serena giggled. "I am here." Proudly she stretched out her hand to the two spotlessly clean rooms. "This is our home."

"It's your very special home," Libby answered, remembering the dirt floor in the one-room cabin where a slave family lived. "Except for your father, you are together."

Again Serena's smile lit her eyes. "Jordan has gone to a meeting at our church."

"And your mother?" Caleb asked. "Captain Norstad wants me to talk to her."

"Momma is working," Serena said. "She is a cook—a very good cook. The lady of the house says Momma is the best cook she ever had. And I clean for them."

"You earn money cleaning?" Libby asked.

"I earn money," Serena said proudly. "Every day I dust the

furniture. The lady of the house says I am the best cleaner she ever had. When I finish work, she gives me and Jordan—"

Serena stopped and corrected herself. "She gives Jordan and me school lessons. Jordan says he's going to learn to talk like Mr. Frederick Douglass."

"Frederick Douglass?" Libby asked, but Caleb knew right away who he was.

"Mr. Douglass is a former slave. He speaks to people all over the country. He traveled to England, speaking there too. Jordan wants to be like him?"

Serena nodded. "Jordan says, 'Now that I is free to learn, I want to sound like I have schooling.' "

"How *is* Jordan?" Caleb asked.

"He helps with the horses. The man of the house says—"

"That Jordan is the best horseman he ever had!" This time Libby giggled.

"Yes'm!" When Serena smiled, a dimple showed in her cheek.

"And your brother Zack?" Libby asked.

"He fishes. He catches big ones." Serena held out her hands as if the fish were monstrous. "And Zack takes care of little Rose when Momma and I work."

Libby smiled, remembering Zack's best friend. The boy had wanted Zack free to go fishing instead of having to work from dawn to dusk.

"Can I talk to your mother, even though she's working?" Caleb asked. "Captain Norstad wants me to ask her a question."

"About my daddy?" The laughter vanished from Serena's eyes. "Momma and Jordan haven't got any word about him. When someone comes to the boardinghouse, the man of the house asks questions for us. He listens. We listen. We haven't got any word."

"And Jordan?" Caleb asked. "Can we talk to him?"

"I'll take you to him."

On their way to the church, Serena told them about the congregation the free blacks of Galena had started some time before. "We have been having bake sales and doing whatever we can to earn money," she explained. "People like our cooking. Every Sunday we take a special offering. That's what the meeting is all about."

"To decide how to spend the money?" Libby asked.

Serena shook her head. "That was settled long ago. That's why we have worked so hard. Tomorrow we are making one more collection. Then someone is going to take all that money to Chicago."

"Why Chicago?" Libby asked.

"John Jones is there," Serena answered as though that explained everything.

"Who is John Jones?" Libby asked.

"A free black," Caleb told her. "He's a tailor and has done very well in business. He and his wife use their big house as an Underground Railroad station. They've taken in countless runaways. He'll probably use the money to buy fares for fugitives who need a boat ride to Canada."

To Canada. Libby had often wondered how fugitives found which boat would help them cross Lake Michigan. And how did captains hide those fugitives from slave catchers?

When they reached the church, Serena led them inside. In the one small room, several men sat on the wooden chairs set up for a meeting.

Sitting in the fourth row back, behind the men, Jordan was the youngest one there. When he saw Libby and Caleb come in, he raised his hand in a quick wave. A grin spread across his face.

The men were still doing business. "It's a mighty big amount of money," said one of them.

"I ain't earned that much in my whole life," answered a heavy-set man as Libby, Caleb, and Serena sat down near the door. "We can be right proud of what we've done."

"Proud and careful," another man answered. "We can't take any chances about what happens to that money."

A white-haired gentleman stood in front of the others, leading the meeting. "The person we send has to carry our gift without anyone knowing how much money he has. He needs to find a safe way to travel so that no one stops him."

Raising his arm, Jordan waved his hand. "I can do it!"

The heavy-set man turned to stare at him. "You're mighty young for a job like this."

"I am young," Jordan admitted. "But I can do it. I led my momma and my sisters and my brother out of slavery."

"That ain't the same as carryin' money," a man growled.

"But I can do it!" Jordan insisted. "I know I can."

At the back of the room Libby looked at Caleb. Being careful not to let Serena see, Caleb shook his head, then whispered in Libby's ear, "No, he can't!"

"What's your plan, Jordan?" asked the white-haired leader.

"Reverend Freeman," Jordan said. "I can travel in the dark of night. I can travel in the heat of the sun. I can get the money to Chicago."

"How are you going to do that?"

"I can walk. I can catch a wagon. I can sneak on board a train."

Reverend Freeman shook his head. "No sneaking for the work of God. If we send you on a train, we give you money for it."

If we send you. Libby's stomach tightened with the dread she felt. How could the church leaders possibly send Jordan? He had never handled money in his whole life.

Then she thought back to the difficult days of May. *Jordan saved the money Pa gave him for working as a cabin boy. Jordan used the money to help his family escape. On the ferry he even paid the fare for Caleb and me. Maybe—just maybe—*

Suddenly Libby felt glad for Reverend Freeman's white hair. *Maybe he's lived long enough to know if Jordan can really do it.*

"Jordan, we all know how you led your momma and your brother and your sisters out of slavery," Reverend Freeman said. "We respect you for it. But don't forget, Chicago is all the way across the state of Illinois. Are you *sure* you can get the money there?"

"I am sure," Jordan answered respectfully. "I can get the money there."

But Reverend Freeman wouldn't let it go at that. "Carrying money offers special temptations," he said. "Temptations about what you could do with all that wealth."

Jordan straightened in the tall, proud look that reminded Libby of royalty. "Reverend Freeman," he said, still respectful. "I ain't weak."

"Jordan, we believe you are a man of God. It is God you honor if you carry this money to Chicago. It is God's money, and you will be helping His people."

Around Jordan the room fell silent as each man turned to look at him. At last someone asked, "Be there any other volunteers?"

When no one answered, Reverend Freeman said, "Then we pray about it."

As one man after another bowed his head, Libby bowed hers also. With all her heart, she wanted to believe in Jordan. But worried thoughts filled her mind. *Caleb doesn't think Jordan can do it. These men—these leaders of the church—are seeking God's help. Does God ever make a mistake? Or could the men make a mistake in knowing what God wants?*

Feeling all mixed up, Libby hoped that someone older and wiser than Jordan would be chosen.

When the men finished praying, Reverend Freeman asked them to speak before he gave his own thoughts. One by one the men said, "Jordan be the person to go."

At last the minister spoke. "Jordan, we have chosen you to take up the call of the Lord. He has called you to keep this money safe, to help our people reach freedom."

From the floor next to his chair, Reverend Freeman picked up a carpetbag. "We have worked many months to collect this great amount of money," he reminded Jordan again.

As if suddenly struck by the seriousness of what he had promised, Jordan's gaze met that of the pastor's. "Yassuh. I'll be very careful, sir."

Reverend Freeman held out the carpetbag. "Take the money

home with you now. Keep it safe, and bring it back tomorrow morning. After we take our last collection, we will send you on your way."

His dark eyes solemn, Jordan took the carpetbag and shook Reverend Freeman's hand. Then Jordan walked back to where Libby, Caleb, and Serena were sitting and led them outside.

They were a block away from the church before Caleb spoke. "Jordan, you can't do this."

Jordan stiffened. "I can't do what?"

"You can't carry all that money to Chicago."

Jordan stopped in his tracks. "You are telling me what I can do?"

"I am telling you that what you've promised to do is very dangerous. It's too big a job."

"All those men in the church said, 'Jordan, you are the one to do this.' "

"But I know you better than any of them," Caleb answered. "I say you can't do it!"

Jordan lifted his head. "You are forgetting something, Caleb Whitney. If I can lead my momma and my sisters and my brother out of slavery, I can do anything!"

"*Anything?*" Caleb asked as though on guard.

"Anything!" Jordan declared. "It ain't just anybody who can do what I did. I am going to keep on doing those big, hard things no one else can do."

"You're sure about that?" Caleb stared at Jordan as if he didn't like what he heard. "Last time I saw you, you were saying humble things about God helping you. Remember?"

Libby remembered, all right. Long ago Jordan's mother had named him after the Jordan River, believing that he would lead his people across the Mississippi into the Promised Land of freedom. To Libby it still seemed a miracle that Jordan had escaped his own cruel master, then led his mother, brother, and two sisters out of slavery.

But Jordan was angry now. "You're forgetting how I led my family in the rain and heat and cold. You are forgetting that my family is here because of what I did!"

Startled, Caleb stepped back, as though he no longer knew his friend. "What did you say you have done?"

"I brought my family out of slavery!"

"*You* brought them here?" Caleb asked.

Jordan threw back his shoulders. "*I* brought them here."

"*Not God?*" Caleb spit out his words. "God didn't help you one bit?"

Jordan blinked. Clamping his mouth shut, he spun around and stalked away.

Turning back, Caleb faced Serena. Gone was the happy smile Libby had seen only a short time before. Instead Serena's eyes flashed with anger.

"You are wrong!" she told Caleb.

As though unable to believe Serena's words, Caleb stared at her.

"You are wrong!" Serena said again. "My brother can do anything!"

5

Peter James Christopherson

Without another word Serena raced after Jordan. Together they hurried down the street. Without speaking, Libby and Caleb watched them go.

Jordan was almost a block away when he suddenly stopped and turned. His shoulders sagging, he walked back slowly. Caleb and Libby met him halfway.

The anger was gone now from Jordan's eyes, but the sureness was still there in the way he held his head. "You are my friends," he said quietly. "You are still my best friends. It would mean something to me if you came to church tomorrow mornin'."

"When the people pray for you?" Caleb asked.

Jordan nodded. As he reached out his hand, Caleb took it, then clapped his friend on the shoulder. Jordan tried to grin, but the troubled look in his eyes did not go away.

When Jordan and Serena left for home a second time, Caleb stood there, as though still shaken by Jordan's words. "I'm scared, Libby," he said finally. "I'm scared about Jordan carrying that much money."

"Scared that he won't make it to Chicago?"

"Scared about a lot of things. Jordan's master, Riggs, might still be looking for him. Wherever there have been posters, slave catchers know about the big reward on Jordan's head. Just because he's been safe in Galena for a few months doesn't mean he'll be safe when he starts traveling again."

Safe. Will Jordan ever be safe? Libby wondered.

During the summer, she and Caleb had vacation from Pa's school lessons. Yet now, like a memory half forgotten, Libby remembered the words he had taught them from the Declaration of Independence: *"We hold these truths to be self-evident, that all men are created equal, that they are endowed by their Creator with certain inalienable Rights, that among these are Life, Liberty and the pursuit of Happiness."*

"The pursuit of happiness," Libby said. "Will Jordan and his family ever be able to pursue happiness without someone pursuing them?"

"There's one thing that scares me more than anything," Caleb answered. "Jordan seems to think he can do big things for God without God's help."

With heavy steps Caleb started back to the riverfront. Walking beside him Libby also felt discouraged. Their visit with Jordan certainly hadn't turned out the way they hoped.

Libby was about to speak when she caught a movement out of the corner of her eye. Turning quickly, she saw a boy in a blue shirt. For an instant he smiled, then disappeared on a side street.

"That's the boy that Samson saved," Libby told Caleb. "I wonder if he lives around here."

But Caleb had no more answers than Libby. Even after she reached the *Christina*, the boy's smile haunted her. As much as she wanted to forget the way he looked, she couldn't.

To Libby's surprise Jordan showed up at the *Christina* an hour later. He no longer carried the carpetbag. At first he walked around between the piles of freight on the riverfront. Then, as if he were part of the crew, he rolled a large barrel up the gangplank. After leaving it on the deck, he headed up the stairs. Libby and Caleb followed him into the captain's cabin.

With the windows and door shut, Jordan told Captain Norstad his problem. "Me and Momma—" Jordan stopped to correct himself. "Momma and I have done our best to find out where my daddy is. We ain't heard even one word about him."

"Sit down, Jordan," the captain said and motioned toward the table where Libby and Caleb had their school lessons.

But Jordan sat on the edge of his chair. "Caleb said you know of a way to find my daddy."

"I do," the captain told Jordan. "But it might bring harm to your entire family."

Jordan leaned forward. "If Daddy is a slave, how can we be happy being free?"

Jordan's words echoed those of his mother, but Libby wondered about them. She remembered the overly confident Jordan she had seen only an hour before. Did he really understand what he was saying?

Captain Norstad's gaze searched Jordan's face. "If we look for your father—doing more than what we've already done in asking questions—do you realize the danger?"

Jordan nodded.

Captain Norstad glanced toward the windows, then lowered his voice. "We can find your father by going to the courthouse in the county where he was sold. His name would be listed there, and the name of his new owner."

A flash of light filled Jordan's face. "That ain't going to be hard," he said with that sure-of-himself voice again.

"But it *will* be hard," the captain warned. "It will be very hard. And you can't be the one going. Someone else needs to ask for you."

"I ain't got no liking for someone else doing it for me," Jordan answered.

"Then we won't do it at all," Captain Norstad answered.

"I want to go myself. I won't have no trouble."

"Jordan . . ." Captain Norstad's eyes were dark with concern. Libby felt sure Pa was going to warn him. But just then Caleb stood up, as if about to take a stroll around the room.

Instead, he stopped next to the door. With one quick jerk he opened it. In the hallway Libby saw a flash of movement as a boy started to run.

But Caleb was faster. Through the open door, Libby saw him catch the boy's arm. A minute later Caleb returned, pulling the boy behind him.

The child looked nine or ten years old. His blond hair fell down over his eyes, reminding Libby of Caleb. To her surprise it was the boy she had seen twice now—the boy Samson had saved from being run over.

"He was listening," Caleb explained. "Standing outside the door as if trying to hear what was going on."

"Is that true?" Captain Norstad asked the boy.

Instead of answering, he looked from one to another, his blue eyes wide with fear.

"Why are you on the boat?" the captain asked.

As though knowing that Captain Norstad had spoken, the boy stared at his face. But he looked puzzled and afraid.

Then Samson stood up from where he lay next to Libby's feet. Walking over to the boy, he lifted one great paw as if to say hello.

For the first time the boy smiled. Taking the paw, he shook it, as though giving his own hello. As he threw his arms around Samson's neck, Libby again noticed his ragged shirt.

"Well, they seem to know each other," Pa said, and Libby explained what had happened. After the near accident, the boy had followed them to where they talked with Jordan, and now here to the *Christina*.

"But he never talks to us," Libby said.

As though afraid that he would frighten him, Pa left his chair and knelt down next to the boy. "What is your name?" he asked.

The boy kept hugging Samson, as if he hadn't heard.

Suddenly it dawned on Libby. "He can talk, but he doesn't

hear! He must have lost his hearing after he learned how to speak!"

Snatching up a slate and a slate pencil from the table, she, too, knelt down next to the boy. Quickly she wrote, then held the slate directly in front of him. "Can you hear?"

After one glance at the words, the boy shook his head.

"No wonder he didn't get out of the way!" Libby exclaimed. "He couldn't hear the horse and buggy coming. Or the driver yelling at him!"

Again she wrote. "Who are you?"

To her surprise the boy smiled and said, "My name is Peter James Christopherson."

Picking up the other two slates on the table, Caleb gave one to Captain Norstad, then sat down on the floor next to Peter. Jordan sat on Caleb's other side. That spring Jordan had asked Caleb to teach him how to read. Every time Caleb wrote something, Jordan watched, as though wishing that he knew enough words to write to Peter.

Libby filled her slate. "How come you have such a long name?"

"Don't let my size fool you," Peter answered. "I've got plenty of brains."

Caleb grinned at Libby. "He's not going to let you get the best of him."

Taking a cloth, Libby erased her words, then wrote again. "Where do you live?"

"With a man who doesn't like me."

"A man who doesn't like you?" Libby glanced toward Pa, not sure that Peter understood what she had asked. Holding out her slate, she again pointed to the words. "Where do you live?"

In reply Peter tapped the words on her slate. "I told you." Taking the slate pencil, he drew a round face with the corners of the mouth pulled down.

"He understood, all right," Caleb said. "I wonder who this man is?"

"Ask Peter why the man doesn't like him," Pa said.

Peter's answer came at once. "He's mean."

"To you?" Caleb wrote.

Peter nodded, as though there was no doubt about it.

"Why?" Caleb asked.

"I am not his boy. He does not like to take care of me."

"Then who takes care of you?" Libby wrote.

"I take care of myself."

Pa groaned. "Ask him more. Who is this man? His uncle? His neighbor?"

To each question Peter shook his head. Finally he said, "The man took me in because my parents died and I didn't have a place to live. Can I live with you?"

Pa took a slate. "Libby is my daughter," he wrote, then pointed to her.

Peter nodded.

Again Pa wrote. "Will you take me to the man you live with? I want to talk with him."

Again Peter nodded.

In a few more minutes, Captain Norstad finished talking with Jordan. "I'll do my best to find your father, Micah Parker," the captain promised before Jordan left. Then Captain Norstad followed Peter down the stairs and off the boat.

Sitting at her favorite place on the hurricane deck, Libby watched them until they disappeared from sight. The entire time they were gone, she kept thinking about Peter's smile—that strange, heartwarming smile that seemed so lonely it made her ache inside.

When Pa returned, Libby and Caleb were both on the hurricane deck where they could look down on the gangplank. Peter had a bag on his back and carried a small carpetbag. It made Libby wonder if that was all Peter owned.

Pa's arms were filled with packages. Soon Libby heard Pa's steps on the stairway. She and Caleb followed Pa to his cabin.

Pa set down the packages on the table. "Clothes for Peter," he explained. "I left him in the pastry kitchen with Caleb's grandmother so I could talk with you."

Pa looked as shaken as Libby had ever seen him. "Peter is an orphan, all right. The man he's living with is self-centered, uncaring, and cruel." Pa's eyes were wet as he told about it. "I don't know how Peter manages the way he does."

"The man is cruel?" Libby asked.

"And rude. When we got to the house, Peter said, 'Wait a minute while I talk to him.' Peter went in while I sat down on the step. The man he lives with never came to the door. Instead he sent a note."

Pa laid a piece of paper down on the table. Libby read the words:

I never wanted Peter in my life. I'm tired of taking care of him. He can go with you for a few trips. For now he's yours.

Libby caught her breath. "Peter's right. The man is mean. I wonder why he took Peter in the first place?"

As Caleb finished reading the note, he turned it over. "Look! Here's more."

Tell Peter to remember what I taught him.

"To remember what he taught him?" Libby asked. "What does the man mean?"

As if wanting to shake off the memory, Pa shrugged his shoulders. "I knocked several times, trying to get him to talk with me, but he wouldn't come to the door. Finally I decided that if someone asks why I have Peter, I'll have this paper."

Pa picked up the piece of paper. "I'll keep it in a safe place. For now I just want to get Peter away from that awful man. I want Peter to grow up living in the sunlight."

So upset that he could not sit still, Pa started pacing around the cabin. It was the way he thought best, Libby knew, and so did Caleb. Without speaking, they waited.

When Pa turned back to them, his mind was made up. "For as long as he's on board, let's be a family for Peter."

"A never-give-up family?" Libby whispered. "A family that sticks together, even when it's hard?"

"A never-give-up family." Pa's voice was rough with emotion. "We're going to love Peter, most of all. We're going to let him tell us what's he's thinking, to break out of that world of silence that he's in. We're going to help him become all that he can be—not for our sake, but for his."

Pa's eyes sought Libby's. "Okay, Libby? Is that all right with you?"

6

The Big Search

Relief washed through Libby—the relief that something good was going to happen to Peter. He would be cared for, fed, and clothed. But it was more than that. After having all the dresses she wanted, Libby had learned how unimportant clothes really were.

With a flash of memory, she thought back four months to the night when her Auntie Vi said, "I'm ready to give up on that girl!"

Give up on me? Libby had felt the pain of those words. From that pain had come her wish for a never-give-up family—a family that believed in her, even if she wasn't perfect.

Since then Pa had shown Libby that he loved her no matter what happened. Could she and Pa give that kind of love to Peter?

Libby looked at Pa. "I've always wanted a younger brother. Even if it's just for a few trips, he could be like a brother."

"I'd like a brother too," Caleb said.

Libby stared at him in surprise. Caleb always seemed so sure of himself and what he wanted. She had never thought about his being an only child too.

The next morning Libby and Caleb set out for the church, with Peter walking between them. On his first night with them, Libby had sewed a small bag for holding a slate. Inside the bag she sewed two narrow pockets for slate pencils.

When she gave the bag to Peter, he taught Libby her first words of sign language—*thank you*. Placing the tips of the fingers of his right hand at the front of his lips, he moved his hand outward, as if blowing kisses to a baby.

Now Peter walked proudly with the new bag slung over his left shoulder, ready to offer the slate if he didn't understand what Libby and Caleb were saying. But Peter was busy teaching them. When he came to a flower, he pointed to it, then showed them the sign. A block farther on, he signed the word for *bird*.

Peter was such a good teacher that it made Libby curious. Taking the slate, she stopped at the side of the street long enough to write to him. "What did the man you stayed with mean when he said, 'Tell Peter to remember what I taught him'?"

As Peter read Libby's words, a shadow seemed to pass over his face. But Peter only said, "He taught me to sell candles on the street. I earned money that way."

When they entered the church, Libby was surprised to see that they were late. Then she realized what had happened. Peter had talked the whole way. Slipping quietly into the back row, Libby, Caleb, and Peter sat down.

Leaning this way and that, Libby managed to see Jordan and his family in the front row. At Jordan's feet lay the cloth bag with handles—the carpetbag with the money the congregation had collected or earned.

Jordan sat tall, as though eager to take on the job he had been given. With all her heart, Libby hoped he was going to succeed. But Caleb seemed strangely quiet, even discouraged. Libby wondered if he was thinking about their talk with Pa last night. When Caleb told him what Jordan had said, Pa had also been concerned.

"I was just about to warn Jordan," he said. "But that's when you heard Peter at the door. Through the terrible days of slavery,

Jordan walked close to the Lord. I hope he doesn't forget God now when life is easier."

Libby hoped so too. More than once Jordan had surprised them by the way he heard God tell him what to do.

Soon Reverend Freeman stood up to speak. "You are not slaves," he told a congregation that Libby knew held many former slaves. "You are created in the image of the almighty God. You are His children!"

Reverend Freeman finished his preaching by saying, "Today we are taking the last offering for our needy people. As they seek the Promised Land, they go with your gifts of love."

After the offering the minister called Jordan forward. "When the leaders met yesterday, we asked the Lord to show us who should take the money to Chicago," he explained to the rest of the congregation. "We agreed on this young man, Jordan Parker."

Suddenly Libby felt proud of Jordan. If the church leaders felt he could succeed in such an important job, surely they knew what they were doing. But Caleb watched without changing his expression. Libby felt impatient with him. Caleb seemed to be looking for trouble.

As the church leaders went forward to pray for Jordan, Reverend Freeman motioned to Hattie and her children. "Come, come. Pray with us for this fine son and brother of yours."

When Hattie stood in front of the congregation, her face glowed with joy. Holding little Rose in her arms, Serena stood next to her mother. She, too, wore a warm glow of pride in Jordan. Zack stood next to his brother, imitating every move that Jordan made. When Jordan clasped his hands behind his back, Zack did too. When Jordan itched his forehead, so did Zack.

As Reverend Freeman began to pray, heads bowed all over the room. His prayer was simple. "Jordan, we send you forth in our good Lord's name. We ask for His protection. We ask for the safe delivery of the money to our needy people. Amen."

At the end of the prayer, some of the leaders stretched out their hands to shake Jordan's. Others clapped him on the shoulder. Jordan grinned, as though eager to be off on his journey.

Taking up the carpetbag, Reverend Freeman held it open for one of the men to place the final offering inside. In that moment the minister looked down. Reaching into the carpetbag, he picked up a bill and read the front side. Even from the back row, Libby saw that his hand trembled.

Looking anxious now, Reverend Freeman pulled out a second dollar bill, then a third, and a fourth. A ripple of concern passed through the congregation.

Libby moaned. "One guess," she muttered to Caleb, feeling as if she'd seen it all before.

Growing more upset by the minute, Reverend Freeman walked over to a table and emptied out the money. Picking up one bill after another, he studied them. Finally he turned to where Jordan and his family still stood at the front of the congregation.

"Jordan, my young friend," the pastor said. "Was this carpetbag ever out of your sight?"

Jordan thought about it. "Yassuh. I left it with Momma when I went down to the river yesterday. And last night one of the maids where Momma works came to our house. She said, 'Come, all of you. The man of the house wants to talk to you.'

"We went to the house and waited in the kitchen. But the man of the house never came. Finally the maid came back and said, 'He can't come now. He will talk to you tomorrow.'

"So Momma said to the maid, 'How come the man of the house told you to get us?' And the maid said, 'He wasn't the one who told me. It was one of the boarders.' "

Suddenly Reverend Freeman pulled out a handkerchief and mopped his forehead. "During that time, the carpetbag was in the carriage house, and no one watching it?"

As if suddenly realizing what had happened, Jordan trembled. "No one was watching it."

"No doors locked?"

"We ain't got no locks."

Jordan's shoulders shook. "Reverend Freeman?" he asked,

his voice filled with fear. "The money?"

Reaching out, Reverend Freeman grabbed hold of the back of a chair. Clinging to the chair, he said, "Someone changed the real money that we saved for wildcat money. The bills in this bag are worthless." Bowing his head, he leaned over the chair as if heartbroken.

As the wave of shock rippled through the room, a cry of anger and unbelief went up from the congregation. People dropped into their chairs.

Softly at first, someone began to weep. Then, with a growing sound, one person, then another sobbed aloud. In that moment Jordan fell on his knees and joined the weeping. But his mother stood tall, her face still, as though unable to take in what had happened.

Then, from the back of the church came an angry voice. "Jordan's family be new here. We ain't got no way of knowin' them!"

From the side of the room came another voice. "How come you gave him the job, anyhow?"

From near the front a man muttered, "We can't trust that Jordan Parker!"

As though new life had come into him, the pastor straightened, facing the congregation. "Can every one of you be trusted? Would you have thought it was safe to leave money in your house when you were right next door?"

A low muttering passed through the room, then silence fell again. His eyes filled with fire, Reverend Freeman spoke again.

"Almost every one of us has been a slave. We have known the whip, the lash upon our back. We have known what it means to be wrongly accused. There will be no accusing word spoken here. There will be no word spoken without proof. No word spoken without love."

In the silence someone began to pray aloud. Soon another voice joined the first, then a third, and a fourth, until the whole room was filled with the sound of people praying. Then, as suddenly as they began, the voices stopped.

A tiny woman walking with a cane came first. Her humped back bowed, she reached out to Hattie with her free hand. Leaning forward, she planted a kiss on Hattie's cheek. Then, still leaning upon her cane, she stopped in front of where Jordan knelt. With her free hand, she reached down, took his hand, and motioned for him to stand.

"Young man," she said in a voice the entire church could hear. "You will still be used of God."

His shoulders bowed, his face wet with weeping, Jordan stared at her. As the little woman walked back to her chair, his gaze followed her dragging steps. When she sat down again, his eyes held the light of hope.

One by one the men and women and children walked forward. Some clasped Hattie's hand. Others reached forward to hug her. But all passed on to Jordan.

One gave a Bible verse, memorized long ago. Another stopped to pray. Men put an arm around Jordan's shoulders.

Then at last Caleb and Libby stood before Jordan. Now that Jordan was in trouble Caleb had a different look on his face. "Do you want Libby and me to help you find the money?" Caleb asked.

"I was proud, wasn't I?" Jordan said when Caleb clapped him on the shoulder. "I ain't proud no more. I need your help."

When the service was over, Jordan faced his pastor. "If I have to leave for a while, I want you to know I ain't running away. Me and my friends are going to find the money."

"If it helps you, some of the bills are marked," Reverend Freeman answered. "When I was counting the money, I spilled a bottle of ink on the table. About ten of the bills have ink blotches on them."

Jordan's voice was humble now. "I want to be the person you think I am," he said.

When Jordan turned to go, Reverend Freeman told him the exact amount of money that had been stolen. "You will find it, Jordan," he said. "You will find the Lord's treasure. You will bring it to our needy people."

For the first time since the discovery of the theft, Jordan straightened, standing tall like royalty.

As Jordan finished talking with people, Libby, Caleb, and Peter went outside.

"Do you think the man who swindled Pa is the one who took Jordan's money?" Libby asked Caleb.

"I wondered about it," Caleb said. "But it seems like such a big coincidence. When Dexter took your pa's money, he was down the river from here. How would he know enough to find Jordan here, unless—"

Libby finished the thought. "Unless he felt sure that sooner or later Pa would come to Galena?"

"Like all steamboat captains do if they travel the Upper Mississippi."

"So if the swindler came to Galena, he just stumbled across Jordan's family?" Libby remembered Dexter shaking his clenched fist at Pa. *"I'll get even with you!"* the swindler had threatened, then seemed to memorize how Jordan looked.

"I'm scared, Caleb," Libby said.

"Me too," Caleb answered to Libby's surprise.

As soon as Hattie came out of the church, she and her family started home. On the way there, Libby and Peter walked behind Caleb and Jordan.

Peter poked Libby to get her attention, then pointed to Jordan. "What happened?"

With all that had gone on, Libby had forgotten that Peter couldn't hear. Taking his slate, she began to write. "Many people gave money to help slaves go on a boat to Canada."

Each time she filled the slate, Peter read what she had written. Libby erased her words, then started writing again. "Jordan was going to take the money to them. But an evil man changed the good money for bad money."

There Peter stopped Libby. "Magician?" he asked.

"No, no!" Libby shook her head.

Peter again pointed to the carpetbag carried by Jordan. "What is bad money?"

Libby sighed. Pa had found it difficult enough to explain to an immigrant. How could she explain to Peter? "Wildcat money," she wrote because she didn't know what else to say.

"Wildcat? Animals don't use money!"

Again Libby shook her head. "Not worth anything," she wrote. "A bad man put worthless money into the carpetbag."

"Swindler?" Peter asked.

Ahhh! Libby felt surprised but nodded yes. How did Peter know about swindlers?

"So all the good money was lost," he said.

Libby nodded.

"Did the church people forgive Jordan?" Peter asked.

Again Libby nodded, but her mind raced ahead. How did Peter know about forgiveness? While living with a cruel man, there must have been many times when Peter needed to forgive. But who had taught Peter how to do it?

"The church people forgave Jordan," Libby wrote, and Peter grinned.

Libby was happy, too, but Peter said, "Now we must find the swindler."

Libby stared at him. Taking the slate, she wrote back. "Peter, how come you're so smart?"

Again Peter grinned. "I will show you a way to say, 'Yes! Yes! You're right!' " Elbows flexed next to his body, he made two fists. As though rooting for someone in a race, he closed his fists. Raising his hands, he brought them forward, then down.

When Libby made the sign after him, Peter nodded his approval. But Libby wrote again.

"I asked, 'How come you're so smart?' "

Instead of answering, Peter took the slate and slipped it into his bag.

As though impatient with how long everyone was taking, Serena half walked and half ran to the boardinghouse. "I want to see if that boarder is still there," she said.

It took only a minute to learn from the owner that the man had left early that morning.

"What was his name?" Caleb asked, but it was one that neither he nor Libby recognized.

"If the boarder took the money, how did he know about it?" Libby asked. "Can we see his room?"

The room the man had rented for one night was on the third floor and faced two directions. One window overlooked the street and the front entrance to the house. The other gave a view across the side lawn to the carriage house where Jordan's family lived.

"Maybe he saw you come home with the carpetbag," Caleb told Jordan, then wrote to Peter.

The ten-year-old had another idea. "Maybe the swindler saw Jordan with the carpetbag, then rented the room."

"Either way, the swindler took a chance," Caleb answered. "And he won."

The room was as clean as if Serena had already dusted every inch of it. "Let's see if the boarder left something," she said.

Every one of them joined in the search. Caleb took down the pictures from the wall, checking the back side to be sure nothing had been hidden. Hattie picked up the rugs, then folded back the quilts and corn-husk mattress. Libby studied the floor inch by inch to be sure there was no hidden crack. Jordan opened every window, testing the movement between the frames and the wall. Serena pulled out each drawer in the dresser, searching behind and underneath.

Finally they had to admit the boarder had left nothing behind.

As they started to leave, Serena turned back. "Wait! There's one more place to look. I've found things there before."

On the far side of the room, a shelf was attached to the wall. Low and strong, it was the kind of shelf where people set their baggage if staying for a short time.

Now Serena peered at a narrow crack between the shelf and wall. Libby could just barely see a narrow edge of paper. Work-

ing carefully so the paper wouldn't slip in farther, Serena managed to pull it out.

The paper had writing on it. Serena tried to read it, then handed it to Libby. There was no name on the paper, but an address in Alton, Illinois.

"It might be just what we need to find the swindler!" Libby exclaimed.

7

Happy Birthday!

"If that address will help us find the swindler, I am going with you," Jordan said.

Then, as if remembering the disaster with the money, he changed his words. "I mean, I am going if your pa lets me work for him again."

As Libby, Caleb, and Peter started back to the *Christina*, Jordan walked with them.

"If we're going to search for the swindler in Alton, maybe I'll have time to find out more about Elijah Lovejoy," Caleb said. More than once he had talked about wanting to be a newspaperman. Mr. Lovejoy had been just that—a newspaper editor who lived at Alton.

Soon Caleb and Jordan walked ahead, talking so fast that Libby knew they were making up for lost time. As she followed with Peter, the boy took out his slate and handed it to her.

"I think I know the man who rented that room," he said.

"You know him? How?" Libby wrote back. Serena had given them a description, but Libby wasn't sure it would be enough to recognize the swindler.

"When your father was taking me to buy clothes, I saw the man walk toward the boardinghouse," Peter said. "I'll take you to where he lives."

"Where he *lives*?" Libby asked, writing again. "Why would he rent a room if he lives in Galena?"

"I told Caleb," Peter said, as though trying to be patient with her. "Maybe the swindler saw Jordan carry the carpetbag and wondered what it held. Maybe he rented the room to find out."

By now Caleb and Jordan were far ahead. Libby called to them. "Stop a minute!"

Peter led them to the house where the man lived, and Caleb knocked on the door. When no one answered, Peter turned the handle, but the door was locked. Carrying his slate with him, he walked around to the back.

As Libby started to follow, she saw Peter talking to a neighbor. Soon Peter returned with words written on the slate. The man Peter thought was the boarder had said he was going away for a while. They had no choice but to start once again for the *Christina*.

"When we get to Alton, we'll try to find the swindler," Libby said.

"You need to know what he looks like," Peter answered. "Brown hair. Blue eyes. About five feet, ten inches tall. He wore a suit and white shirt and tie. A hat too. He dresses good."

"Well dressed, you mean?" Libby wrote.

"But he doesn't know how to wear clothes."

Strange, Libby thought. *What does Peter mean by that?*

Peter explained. "He has money but hasn't learned to dress like he is rich."

"Have you seen such a man?" Libby asked Jordan.

He hadn't, but according to Serena, the boarder had taken meals in his room during his one-night stay. It would have been easy for him to keep out of Jordan's sight.

"When we go to Alton, you will be the only one who can identify the thief," Libby told Peter. "How can we thank you enough?"

"You better learn to sign what you want to say," Peter answered, and Libby wasn't sure if he was teasing or not. Soon she found out.

"Your name," Peter said. "*L* for Libby."

Watching closely, Libby learned how to sign the letter *L*. Pointing to Jordan, Peter made the sign for *J*, then a *C* for Caleb.

When they reached the *Christina*, Jordan talked with Pa about what had happened. Captain Norstad told him, "Yes, you can work for me again." Jordan returned home long enough to say good-bye to his family.

The next morning the *Christina* again steamed down the Galena River. Libby and the three boys met with Pa in his cabin. Caleb sat next to Peter, explaining on a slate.

"We have three problems now," Captain Norstad told Jordan. "Finding your father, finding the man who stole money from your church, and finding the man who robbed me."

Four problems, Libby thought, then guessed that Pa didn't want to mention his need to make a double payment on a loan by August fifteenth.

The July day was warm and humid, and the windows in Pa's cabin were open. For a moment he walked around, looking through the windows as though making sure that no one hid on the deck to listen. Then he returned to where the rest of them sat at the table.

"Word has gotten around about how you rescued your family," the captain told Jordan. "It will be an especially dangerous time to ask about your father."

Jordan nodded, as though he understood the risks.

But then Pa said, "When we get close to the county in which your father was sold, you need to hide."

Clearly Jordan was disappointed. "Who will do the asking at the courthouse?"

"Not Captain Norstad," Caleb said quickly. "If the wrong

person sees him there, it could wreck everything he's doing to help runaway slaves."

Pa agreed. "Slave catchers will search the *Christina* even more than they do now. Caleb needs to be the one who asks."

"Caleb?" Libby asked. Deep inside she felt scared just thinking about the danger.

But Jordan objected. "Captain Norstad, slave catchers know Caleb. They know what he's up to. If they recognize him, they'll be watching him every second."

"That's why I'm leaving the decision up to Caleb and his grandmother. It's impossible for you to go, Jordan. But it's almost as dangerous for him."

The captain turned to Caleb. "Before we get there, I want you and Gran to agree on what you should do."

Then he changed the subject. "We have a number of stops on the way down the river. Tomorrow night we'll tie up in Hannibal, Missouri. On Wednesday morning, before first light, we'll start our celebration of Libby's thirteenth birthday."

"My birthday?" Until now Pa hadn't spoken a word about it. The way Caleb looked, she suspected he already knew Pa's plans. But neither he nor Pa would tell her more.

"Don't be surprised if Caleb's grandmother wakes you up when it's still dark," Pa told Libby.

"So Gran is in on it too?" Libby could hardly wait for her big day.

In the early morning hours, Libby heard a quiet rap on the door of her room, then the soft voice of Caleb's grandmother. "Happy birthday, Libby."

Kneeling on her bed, Libby reached out to open the door.

"Are you awake?" Gran asked as she came in. "It's your special day!"

"I'm awake." Libby's voice was groggy, but then she remembered. "It really *is* my birthday!"

Because of the danger of fire, Libby wasn't allowed to have a lamp in her room. In the darkness she heard Gran set a pitcher of water on the washstand in the corner.

As Libby yawned and stretched, the corn husks in her mattress crackled. When Gran left, Libby bounded out of bed. She didn't want to waste one moment of this special day.

The warm water felt good on her face and arms. As soon as she finished washing, Libby put on her favorite dress. Though she could not see herself in the mirror, she knew the soft green brought out the honey color in her skin. Brushing her deep red hair, she pulled up the front strands, tying them in place with a ribbon.

When Libby reached the main deck, passengers were still sleeping wherever they had found a place to lie down. At the bottom of the steps Pa waited in the dark. When his arm circled her shoulders in a quick hug, he whispered, "Happy Birthday, Libby!"

"Where are we going, Pa?" she whispered back, but he wouldn't tell her.

As Libby crossed the deck, Peter was ahead of her. At the gangplank he stopped, as if not sure whether he should walk down.

"Go ahead, Peter," Libby said softly, then remembered he couldn't hear.

Instead of moving on, Peter held back. Then, as if offering a special escort for Libby's birthday, he turned to her and held out his arm. When she took it, he walked sideways down the gangplank.

Gran, Caleb, and Jordan stood next to a team of horses and a wagon. Gran climbed up to the high seat next to Pa, and Libby and the boys sat on the straw in the back of the wagon. As it rolled through the streets of Hannibal, Libby saw the darkness of night beginning to fade.

Before long the wagon rumbled over a bridge, then tilted upward when the horses started up a long hill. In the grayness before dawn, Pa drove the horses off the road and halted them near the beginning of a trail.

Now Libby was really curious. With her eyes used to the dusky light, she had no problem seeing the way. But why was Pa taking them here? And what did this have to do with her birthday?

With Pa leading, the rest of them followed single file. As they walked, the rough trail grew more and more steep. Now and then they stopped to rest, and Caleb's grandmother breathed deeply to catch her breath. Gran was at least fifteen years older than Pa, and it was a difficult climb for persons of any age.

When they reached a large mound, they followed the trail along its side to the top of the bluff. In the half-light only moments before dawn, Libby turned toward the river. A short distance from where she stood, the mound sloped down to a large, flat rock. Jutting out like a shelf, the rock fell sharply away for two hundred feet.

Taking Libby's hand, Pa led her to a safe distance from the edge. As the others gathered around, Libby stared at the enormous drop in front of her. Her heart pounding, she wanted to turn and run in the opposite direction.

Pa doesn't know my fear of heights, Libby thought. Panic washed over her, and she felt as if she were falling forward.

In that moment her father squeezed her hand. Libby's world steadied, and she saw beyond the jagged rock. Stretched out before her lay the great Mississippi River and its wide valley.

"Look!" Pa said, and with his words, Libby forgot her fear.

Far across the silvery water, beyond the hills six miles away, rose-colored light spread above the line of trees. Without speaking, Libby watched the water turn pink. Above the river, clouds, like puffs of cotton, caught the changing light.

As the color swept around her, Libby turned slowly, and the others turned with her. In the north, south, and even the western sky, thin bands of clouds reflected the rose light. Never in all her life had Libby seen anything like the glory of that sunrise.

Then, as golden light spread upward, the pink faded. The top arc of the great orange ball that was the sun appeared above the horizon.

"It's the dawning of your thirteenth birthday," Pa said quietly. "Happy birthday, Libby."

Thirteen! Libby wanted to sing, to dance, to shout—to tell the whole world, "I'm almost grown up!"

Then she remembered. *I've never been thirteen before. What will it be like? How will this year be different from any other year of my life?*

I'm not a little girl anymore. Yet when Libby looked ahead to being a woman, she felt scared.

As she thought about how Pa had planned this moment for her, Libby's throat tightened. Blinking away her tears, Libby squeezed his hand back. "Thank you, Pa."

Without speaking, she and the others stood there as the orange light moved upward. When the sun grew too bright to watch, Libby looked out over the streets and buildings of Hannibal. From where she stood, the *Christina* looked like a small white toy—a plaything a child could float in any puddle of water. But for Libby the *Christina* was home.

Down the river, then up, Libby's gaze followed the shoreline. By the time she turned to leave, the sun had cast a pathway of light across the waters of the Mississippi. Standing on the great jagged rock a final time, Libby watched the waves ripple against the shore far below them.

I'll never forget seeing the sun rise on my thirteenth birthday, she thought. *Best of all, the people I love most are gathered around me.*

At the bottom of the bluff again, they drove to a grove of trees called Cave Hollow. When Caleb carried a large picnic basket from the wagon, Gran spread a tablecloth on the grass and set out the food.

As everyone sat down around the cloth, Pa again reached out his hand to Libby. One by one they clasped hands until the circle was complete.

Bowing his head, Pa started to pray. "We thank you, Father, that you are the one who created Libby. You are the one who gave her this special day. As the sun rises upon her thirteenth birthday, we ask you to watch over her. Care for her, protect her, give her your love. And most of all, Lord, help her to become strong in you."

When the silence grew long, Libby looked up to find Pa looking at her.

"In the name of our Lord, we bless you, Libby." His voice was husky with emotion.

As Libby looked around the circle, the warm feeling of being loved filled her to overflowing. *Pa. Caleb. Gran. Jordan. And now Peter. My never-give-up family,* Libby thought. *We don't always agree, but we stick together. No matter what happens, we're a family.*

Then, seeing Peter, Libby remembered that she had forgotten to talk on his slate. Did he understand what was going on?

When Peter grinned at her, Libby knew. Though he hadn't heard every word, he understood.

Gran began offering food: boiled eggs still in the shell, slices of fresh peaches, golden pears, and the cinnamon rolls that Libby loved.

As they were eating, Libby felt curious. Caleb was thirteen, almost fourteen now, and Peter had told Libby he was ten. But what about Jordan?

"How old are you?" Libby asked him.

Jordan was enjoying his food so much that when he shrugged his shoulders, Libby thought he didn't want to stop eating.

"Thirteen? Fourteen?" Libby asked.

Again Jordan shrugged.

"When's your birthday?"

This time Jordan looked directly at her. "I ain't got no idea."

Libby stared at him. How could someone possibly not know his own birthday?

"Momma didn't have any way of knowing the day I was born," Jordan explained. "And she didn't know how to write it down. Momma said Old Master put it in his book."

"Serena?" Libby asked, even more curious now. "Does Serena know when her birthday is?"

Jordan shook his head.

"Zack?"

Again Jordan shook his head.

"Little Rose?"

Jordan grinned. "Rose was born when the roses bloomed."

"Do you know the time of year you were born?" Libby asked.

"Momma said it was before the time of harvest. Before the corn was bending down, ready to be picked."

"Then could it be a day in September?" Libby asked. "You decide when, and we'll celebrate."

But Jordan once again shook his head.

"You don't want to celebrate your birthday?" Libby asked.

Jordan's eyes were solemn now—dark and deep with how strongly he felt. "I want my birthday to be the day I know my daddy is free."

8

Jordan's Daddy

Libby ate until she was full, then began opening her gifts. Gran had sewed her a new skirt. From Pa came new drawing pencils and paper. Jordan gave her a half-open clam shell—clean, polished, and beautiful. And from Peter, a drawing of a sunrise and the words, *Happy birthday, Libby*.

When there were no more gifts to open, Libby looked up to find Caleb watching her. "I'll have a present for you later," he said, and Libby could only feel curious.

As she and the others returned to the *Christina*, Caleb told her more. "I'll give you my present as the sun sets on your thirteenth birthday."

The sun was low in the sky when Caleb found Libby sitting near the bow of the *Christina*. On the deck around them, other people talked together or played games.

"Your pa has business in Hannibal," Caleb said. "We're not leaving till sometime tonight."

Caleb kept one hand behind him. When he sat down on a nearby crate, Libby knew he had hidden something behind his back, for his hand came out empty.

What is it? she wondered as she had all day. She could hardly wait to find out.

For Libby half the fun of the day was remembering all that had happened. In her mind's eye, she could still see the sun rising on her thirteenth birthday.

"That was Illinois you were looking at," Caleb reminded her as Libby described the view across the river.

Only once did they talk about what would happen the next morning. "What are you going to do about finding Jordan's father?" Libby asked.

But Caleb shook his head, not wanting to talk about it. "Don't spoil your birthday."

The sun had dropped behind the hills of Hannibal when Libby spoke again. "Caleb, I'm scared about you going to that courthouse. I'm scared that someone will recognize you, that he'll accuse you of helping slaves and have you thrown in jail."

"Shhh!" Caleb said. "The sun is setting. I said I'd give you your present now." Looking half embarrassed, Caleb reached behind his back and handed her a gift.

When Libby took the package, she felt the weight of it. Then, as the wrapping paper fell away, she understood why Caleb didn't want her to open his gift in front of the others. In the center of a piece of carefully sanded pinewood, Caleb had carved letters. With a reddish stain made from berries along the river, he had colored each letter:

THE LORD IS MY LIGHT
AND MY SALVATION;
WHOM SHALL I FEAR?
—Psalm 27:1

Libby caught her breath. Never had she seen anything so beautifully carved. Yet it was more than that. "The Lord is my light," she said. "He leads me and shows me the way. But He's also my salvation."

As clearly as if it happened only moments before, Libby thought back to the spring day when she nearly died. Because of that life-and-death moment, she knew how much she needed Jesus.

"It was a miracle, wasn't it?" Libby asked, thinking about that time. "Remember our walk along the river and how I almost drowned?"

Caleb nodded.

"Remember how we talked around the campfire? I asked Jesus to forgive my sins. He gave me His forgiveness. I asked for His salvation, and He gave me His peace. My life has been different ever since."

Now Caleb had given her a promise she could repeat to herself and remember. In the last light of the sun, Libby traced each letter with a finger. When she finally looked up, she found Caleb watching her.

"Thank you," Libby said softly. "I will treasure your gift forever. When I need to remember what Jesus has done, I'll think of the words."

"There's more to the verse," Caleb told her. " 'The Lord is the strength of my life; of whom shall I be afraid?' "

As he and Libby talked, the sky grew dark. On the deck around them, people talked less, then fell silent.

"You know," Caleb said. "I'm glad you want to work with the Underground Railroad."

His words surprised Libby. When she first met Caleb, he had tried to keep her from taking part. "Why do you say that?" she asked.

"It's good to be friends," Caleb answered.

Libby's heart leaped. "Yes, it's good to be friends."

Far above them the stars appeared, twinkling in the night sky. Libby yawned and stretched, then stood up to leave.

"It's been a perfect day," she said. "Thanks for everything."

Starting up the wide stairs at the front of the boat, she thought again about all that had happened from the moment Gran woke her until now. Libby wanted to hug this time to herself and remember it as the most wonderful day of her life.

When she reached the texas deck, she started toward her

cabin. Just then she heard a noise from somewhere close by. Standing in the dark, Libby listened, then moved toward the sound. It seemed to be a soft sniffling, as if the person was trying to hide how he felt.

What is it? Someone crying?

At the back end of the boxlike structure called the texas, a stairway led to the pilothouse. As Libby rounded the corner, she saw a small light beneath the steps.

Uh-oh! Libby thought. *Is that fire I see?*

Quietly she crept closer. *Peter! Sitting in the dark with a candle!*

When Libby suddenly appeared in front of him, he jumped. Eyes wide with fear, he almost dropped the candle.

"What are you doing?" Libby asked, then remembered he couldn't hear.

Peter's slate lay on the deck beside him. Picking it up, Libby tipped the slate toward the moon and started writing. "You can't have a candle. It's against the rules."

Holding out the candle, Peter read what she said. Drops of wax fell on Libby's words. That upset her even more.

"Rules?" Peter asked.

"Rules of the boat," Libby wrote. "Because of the danger of fire, Pa does not allow us to have candles or matches up here."

As soon as Peter read what she said, Libby stretched out her hand. But Peter shook his head, as if he didn't understand.

Libby took the slate again. "Give me your candle and matches. You can't have them."

Still looking confused, Peter jumped up.

As though repeating her words, Libby tapped the slate. "Give them to me!"

Instead Peter backed away. When Libby started after him, he blew out the candle and began to run. In the darkness he stumbled, falling the two steps to the hurricane deck.

Stopping in her tracks, Libby panicked. The railing around the hurricane deck was low. *What if Peter falls over?*

Just then Caleb came up the stairway from the boiler deck. As Peter picked himself up, he ran into Caleb.

"Hey! What's wrong?" Caleb asked.

"Hang on to him!" Libby exclaimed. Whirling around, she stomped across the texas deck to Pa's cabin.

When she threw open the door, she found Pa sitting in his big chair. With his first look at Libby he stopped rocking.

"That boy you took into our family just wrecked a perfect day!" Libby sputtered.

"What's wrong?" Pa asked as Caleb and Peter appeared at the door.

"I was just coming to talk to you, when Peter ran into me," Caleb said. "For some reason he carries a candle in his pocket. A candle wrapped up in a waterproof cloth."

"Well, that's not so serious." Pa looked to Libby. "What's really bothering you?"

"Peter also carries matches." Libby spit out her words.

"Matches?"

"And he uses them."

"That *is* serious," Pa said.

"I found Peter sitting under the stairs to the pilothouse. He was holding a lighted candle. When I told him you don't allow us to have matches and candles, he ran away from me."

Pa sighed. Standing up, he walked over to Peter. Holding out his hand, he motioned to a chair, and they all sat down around the table.

Taking a slate, Pa started writing. "Peter, why did you light a candle?"

"To see in the dark," Peter said.

"That's a good reason," Pa wrote. "But the wind might catch the flame and start a fire."

When Peter looked from one to another, Pa wrote again. "Do you understand?"

"I understand I must be careful not to start a fire," Peter answered.

"Good," Pa said, then remembered to write. "Give me your candle and matches."

Slowly, as if he were giving up his prized possession, Peter took the candle from his pocket.

"And the matches," Pa wrote.

As though not wanting to obey, Peter hesitated. But Pa waited. Finally Peter gave him the matches.

Watching them, Libby felt proud of herself. *I stopped something really serious,* she thought. *Maybe I even saved the* Christina.

But when Peter left the cabin, he walked with his head bowed.

Something bothers him much more than being caught, Libby thought. Only then did she remember that she had found Peter crying. Libby sighed. *I had to tell Pa. But maybe I could have found a better way.*

That night Libby woke to hear the engines throbbing and the paddle wheels slapping the water as the *Christina* steamed downriver. The next morning Pa and Caleb talked again about his going to the courthouse in the county where Jordan's father was sold. As Libby stood with them on the hurricane deck, the sunlight felt warm and cheerful. But Libby already felt cold with dread about what could happen to Caleb.

"You know there might be a cost to your doing this," Pa warned him.

Caleb straightened. "I know, sir."

"And you want to do it anyway?"

"I want to go anyway."

"You've prayed about it?"

"Yes, sir. Ever since you told me there was a way for Jordan to find out about his father. When I prayed about it, I found a Bible verse that was so real it seemed to jump off the page."

In that moment Libby felt sure she knew what verse God had made real to Caleb. Looking up, she saw Caleb watching her again. As she wondered if he knew what she was thinking, her face grew warm with embarrassment.

"Dress up in your Sunday suit," the captain warned Caleb.

"Walk into the courthouse as if you know what you're doing. Act as if you have the right to ask."

Then, as soon as Pa prayed for him, Caleb disappeared into his room.

Half an hour later, when the *Christina* tied up at the riverbank, Libby watched from the hurricane deck. As soon as the gangplank went down, Caleb left the boat.

In his suit, white shirt, and tie, he looked at least two years older than his age. Deep inside, Libby felt a warm glow that she could be his friend. Whenever Caleb let her be a part of his life and his work for the Underground Railroad, Libby felt proud that she knew him.

But now it was Caleb's role in that secret plan that worried Libby. Over the years slave catchers in southeastern Iowa and parts of Missouri had started to find out what Caleb was doing. Wherever he was recognized, catchers watched him closely. Often Libby wondered, *What would happen if Caleb were caught with a runaway slave? Would he be treated like an adult and sent to jail?*

A short distance beyond the piles of freight on the riverfront, Caleb turned around. When he looked up, Libby knew he expected to find her there. As though rooting for someone in a race, Libby closed her fists in Peter's sign. Raising both hands, she brought them forward, then down. When Caleb signed back, Libby returned his grin.

He looks excited, Libby thought. *Excited and happy that he can do something to help Jordan's family.* Sometimes Libby thought that Caleb thrived on danger, and maybe he did. In those moments of quick, difficult choices, he always seemed at his best.

Hour after hour Libby waited for Caleb to return. When morning turned into afternoon, she saw that even Pa looked worried. Finally Libby went to her room high on the texas deck. On her desk was the plaque Caleb had given her. As Libby picked it up, Peter knocked on the door.

"What's it say?" he asked when Libby held the plaque so he couldn't see.

At first Libby didn't want to show it to him. Then she remembered the way she treated Peter the night before. When she turned the plaque for him to see, he read the words aloud, as if it were a favorite verse.

"I'll teach you signs for the first part," he offered, and Libby followed him out to the deck.

"First word," said Peter, pointing to the word *Lord*. With the thumb and index finger on his right hand, he made an *L*. With his palm facing out, he touched his thumb to his chest about four inches from his left shoulder. As though he were a king wearing a ribbon filled with medals, he drew the *L* down across his chest to his right hip.

"Lord," Peter said again, as if wanting to be sure Libby understood.

Again he pointed to the plaque. "Second word. *My*." His fingers together, Peter held the flat palm of his right hand against the center of his chest.

"Third word. *Light*."

With both hands near his chest, Peter held the thumb and fingers of each hand together, as though ready to pick up grains of sand from a beach. Slowly spreading wide the fingers on both hands, he gradually stretched out his arms until both hands were high above his head.

Like the rays of the sun, Libby thought, deeply moved. *Like the sun rising on my birthday.*

"The Lord is my light," she said softly. Peter seemed to read her lips, for he nodded.

As he repeated all the motions, Libby watched carefully until she could do them herself. Then she remembered to write, "Peter, were you crying last night?"

The ten-year-old ducked his head, and Libby knew he didn't want to talk about it. Was he lonely for his parents?

When Peter left, Libby went back to her room. She felt restless, worried, unable to think about anything except what was happening to Caleb. Then as she set down the plaque he had given her, Libby felt ashamed. *Already I've forgotten the promise. Already I've forgotten that it's you, God, who takes care of Caleb.*

More than once Libby had seen Jordan get down on his knees to pray. Suddenly Libby found herself next to her bed on her knees, her face in the quilt. Her prayers began with telling God how scared she felt about Caleb. But slowly, gradually, peace crept into her heart. One thought became real—the promise of the Lord as her light and her salvation.

When at last Libby stood up, she had no doubt that her trust in God would be tested again. She had no doubt that fear would again knock on the door of her heart. But now, in this moment, something in her life had changed.

As she brushed her deep red hair, the sun shining through the window brought out the gold highlights. In the mirror Libby saw the glow in her face. "*You,* Lord, are my light and my salvation," she whispered.

When Caleb finally returned to the *Christina,* he, too, saw the change in Libby. For the first time he told her, "Thanks for praying for me."

Once again they gathered around the table in the captain's cabin—Caleb, Jordan, Peter, Pa, and Libby. Caleb's eyes sparkled with success, yet Libby also caught a deeper look of something else.

"When I asked about Jordan's father, the man in the courthouse told me the name and address of Micah Parker's new owner. He also said that the owner lived nearby."

In the same way that Pa had checked a few nights before, Caleb walked over to the windows and searched the deck just outside. With Libby writing for Peter, Caleb went on with his story.

"I started suspecting something because of the way the man in the courthouse acted. When I asked a question, I spoke in a quiet voice. When he answered, he spoke in a loud voice. Heads turned, and a rough-looking man crowded close.

"I left, thinking I'd ask directions from someone else. But the rough-looking man followed me. I had to shake him before I did anything else.

"For a while I hid out between two warehouses. From there

I could see the man looking around, as though wondering where I'd gone. Before long he met a man I haven't seen before.

"While they were talking, I slipped away and got the directions I needed. Micah Parker's master owns a number of really good horses, and Micah took care of them."

Libby caught the change in Caleb's story. "*Took* care of them?" she asked. "He doesn't take care of them now?"

"Nope. As I watched the stable, I saw an eight- or nine-year-old boy go inside. He seemed to be a young slave who worked there. I crept close and asked him, 'Do you know Micah Parker?' The boy looked scared.

" 'I don't know nothin' about him!' he said.

" 'Nothing?' I asked. I knew the boy was lying because he was afraid. 'I'm Micah Parker's friend,' I said, but he didn't trust me. He kept edging away, and I knew he'd run at any moment.

"Finally I said, 'Micah Parker's son Jordan is my friend.'

"The minute the boy heard Jordan's name, he looked around to be sure no one could hear. Then he whispered, 'Micah always told me he was goin' to find his family. Tell Jordan his daddy ran away last night.'

" 'He got away?' I whispered back.

" 'Yassuh. I heard the dogs bark.' "

Suddenly Jordan broke into Caleb's story. "I am going there! I am going to find that stable boy and find which way my daddy went!"

"You can't go there," Caleb answered. "If the wrong person sees you, that's the end of your freedom."

"I ain't going to let nobody see me."

"Shush!" Caleb said, and went on. "Then the stable boy told me, 'I heard the dogs goin' toward the river. When the men came back, they be hoppin' mad. Master called out even more men—biggest bunch I ever seed. They searched up and down the river, but no boat were there. Toward sunup they came back too. One of them said, 'I bet that Micah drowned.' "

9

Secret in the Rock

"Drowned?" Captain Norstad looked at Jordan, a worried frown on his face.

But Jordan surprised them with a grin. "My daddy didn't drown. Ain't nobody who can swim the way he can. If he was near the river, he crossed it."

"Your daddy could swim across the Mississippi River?" Libby asked. "How come he didn't teach you?" More than once it had been a problem that Jordan didn't know how to swim.

"No lake or river or crick where we were livin'," Jordan said. "Daddy always told me, 'Jordan, the minute we get near water, I am going to make a swimmer out of you.' But my daddy was sold away."

"So maybe your father really did escape," Captain Norstad said. "Around here there are a lot of islands in the river. He could swim from one to another."

"Yassuh." Jordan seemed to have no doubt in his mind. "What happened next?" he asked Caleb.

"The stable boy said, 'Today I heard a poundin' on that tree down the road.' He pointed to a large oak. 'Can you read?' he asked. 'Maybe that paper will tell you what you wants to know.'

"There were a hundred things I wanted to ask," Caleb said. "But I knew if someone found the boy talking to me, he'd be whipped. So I crept away. The reward poster was about Micah Parker, all right. There's an even bigger reward for him than for you," Caleb told Jordan.

Again Jordan grinned, as though enjoying the story of his daddy's escape. "Us Parkers have value, all right. There ain't nobody who knows horses the way my daddy does."

"When I started back to the *Christina,* I kept looking around," Caleb went on. "Several times I hid along the way to see if someone would pass me. Once I saw a man jump out of sight, so I used every trick I know to lose someone."

Caleb looked tired, and now Libby knew why the day had grown so long.

"I was sure I had shaken the person following me," Caleb went on. "So I hurried on board the *Christina.* But when I slipped down behind some freight, I looked back. Just then I saw that rough-looking man who was in the courthouse."

"He followed you all that way?" Captain Norstad was concerned. "To where Jordan's father lived and back?"

"Maybe," Caleb answered. "Maybe not. The man he was talking to could have recognized me. If he knew what boat I was from, we're in trouble."

Captain Norstad agreed. "Since you went there about the time Jordan's father escaped, they might think you had something to do with it."

Standing up, Captain Norstad left to give orders. Already the *Christina* had her steam up so she could leave on a moment's notice.

Going out on the hurricane deck, Libby lay down on her stomach and peered through the railing. Within a few minutes, deckhands took in the lines, and the *Christina* blew her departing whistle. Watching the waterfront, Libby tried to spot anyone who might be watching. If someone was there, he was well hidden.

Soon Caleb, Jordan, and Peter joined Libby on the deck. As the *Christina* steamed downstream, the Illinois River flowed into the Mississippi, creating an even wider expanse of water. Whenever Libby saw one of the many islands dotting the river, she wondered, *Is Jordan's father hiding there? Or did he make it all the way across?*

Even if Micah Parker stopped at the islands, the current in the river was strong. No doubt about it, if Jordan's father crossed around here, he had to be a very good swimmer.

Or desperate. As if a cold chill had crept into the hot July wind, Libby shivered.

"As soon as we get to Alton, I'll start asking questions," Caleb promised Jordan. "We'll find out if your father went through there. And we'll check that address Serena found. Maybe we'll find the swindler too."

"But how are we going to find my daddy?" Jordan asked.

"If we take an Underground Railroad route, we might find someone who has seen him."

When Captain Norstad returned, he knelt down on the deck behind them and spoke in a low voice. "Caleb, you're heading into the most dangerous situation you've had yet. More important than any money is the life of Micah Parker. If he was able to cross the river, he'll find the Underground Railroad. As dangerous as that is, there's something worse."

Captain Norstad waited until each of them turned to face him. "If you ask questions about Jordan's father and the wrong person hears, you'll put Micah's life in danger. And Jordan might be taken back into slavery."

The captain looked from one to the other. "Don't forget. At Alton you'll be only twenty-three river miles away from where Jordan escaped."

Instead of north-to-south, this part of the Mississippi flowed from west to east. Tall limestone bluffs rose sharply upward on the Illinois side of the river. As the *Christina* drew close to the city of Alton, Libby gazed at the rugged hillside, the gray stone walls of the prison, and the warehouses hugging the shore. Now, with a deeper understanding of what they meant, she felt drawn to the church steeples rising above the other buildings.

Soon the *Christina* nosed alongside the large flat rock that formed a natural wharf. There was no freight waiting for Pa.

As usual, he did not complain, but Libby saw the expression on his face. Another steamboat had no doubt arrived just before them, taking all the freight and passengers headed for St. Louis. It cost money to run with a half-empty boat, and that was happening to Pa on this trip.

August fifteenth, Libby thought, no longer able to push away her worry. *Today is Thursday, July thirtieth. The deadline for Pa's loan is only sixteen days away. If only we could find the money stolen from Pa and from Jordan.*

"I don't want to leave you here," Pa said when he told Libby he had to keep going to St. Louis to pick up freight and passengers. "But I don't have any choice. I'll come back as soon as I can."

"We'll find an Underground Railroad conductor quickly enough," Caleb told him.

Pa grinned. "I'm sure you will. If you have to leave town, leave word for me at the *real* depot." The building where people waited for the St. Louis, Alton and Chicago trains was about five or six blocks from the river.

Then Pa grew serious. "Libby, you be responsible for Peter, okay?"

When she nodded, Pa went on. "All of you need to promise me one thing. If you find the swindler, get help from a grown-up—a policeman or sheriff. Someone like that."

Like Caleb, Jordan, and Peter, Libby carried a few extra clothes in a cloth bag on her back. When the others started to leave, Libby stayed behind to give her own good-bye to Pa.

"You know how you talked about Peter needing sunlight?" she asked him. "There's something dark in his life. Something I don't understand."

"Maybe that's what I was trying to say about wanting him to grow up in the sunlight," Pa said. "When we know Peter better, we might discover all kinds of secrets—things that are much harder than being deaf."

As Libby stepped down on the wharf, she felt empty in the pit of her stomach. Whenever Pa was around, life seemed safe and filled with love, no matter what happened. Now she hated to see him leave.

Turning, she waved to her father, then followed the boys to the riverbank. As always when Caleb slipped into his Underground Railroad role, he strolled along, looking as if nothing important were happening. But Libby knew better. Only four months before, Jordan had escaped to this very city to make his way onto the *Christina*.

Pausing here, then there, Caleb kept walking. When he and Jordan stopped at the great piles of wood used for fuel on steamboats, Jordan suddenly disappeared. *Now how did he do that?* Libby wondered.

For a moment she stopped next to Caleb. "Peter and I are going to the depot," she said, knowing that Caleb could ask more questions without her.

When Libby and Peter headed for the Alton railroad depot, they had their first taste of climbing the steep hills. Once, Libby stopped to catch her breath. Before long she felt the tug of muscles at the back of her legs. By the time she and Peter reached the depot, those muscles ached.

The depot was built of huge limestone blocks three feet thick. As in most stations of that time, one waiting room was set aside for men, another for women and children. But Peter found his way into a smaller room.

A man sat at a desk, using a telegraph. As his finger jiggled a lever, Libby heard short and long clicks and knew she was hearing Morse code, a dot-dash way of communicating. Though Peter could not hear the clicks, his gaze was glued to the telegraph operator and what he was doing.

"Telegraph," Libby wrote on the boy's slate. She herself had seen a telegraph only a few times before.

"I know," Peter said.

More than once Libby had felt surprised by all that Peter knew. Wherever he went, Peter watched every move that people made.

When Libby wanted to leave, Peter wanted to stay. The third time she tugged on his arm, he said, "Samuel Morse has a deaf wife."

Libby stared at him. "You're sure?" Then she remembered to shrug her shoulders and raise her eyebrows as if in a question.

Taking one of Libby's hands, Peter held it palm up. Using two fingers, he began tapping into her palm.

"That's how they talked?" Libby asked. "That's how he got the idea for the Morse code?" Then she remembered to write.

As Peter nodded, his grin stretched from ear to ear. A moment later he suddenly turned his back on the operator. Edging close to Libby, Peter stood between her and a man who had entered the room. When Libby would have spoken, Peter put a finger across his lips as though to say, "Shhh!"

Without giving Libby a chance to speak, Peter grabbed hold of her arm. Still with his back toward the man, he guided Libby through another door into a waiting room. From there he hurried Libby outside and around part of the building.

Libby felt more impatient by the minute. First Peter hadn't wanted to leave. Now with no reason at all, he dragged her away. But when she tried to complain, his grip tightened on her arm. Again he laid his finger across his lips.

Only then did Libby see what Peter was doing. While standing out of the direct view of anyone in the building, Peter looked through a window into the telegraph office. "Danger!" he whispered.

Libby's heart lurched. She wrote on Peter's slate. "The swindler?"

Leaning forward, she looked beyond Peter into the room. No doubt about it, the man fit the exact description Peter had given her in Galena. As the man talked to the telegraph operator, Libby studied the swindler. *Brown hair. Blue eyes. Broad back. About five feet, ten inches tall.*

Peter was right in yet another way. The man had money, yes. Libby knew enough about clothes to guess how much he had spent on them. But he didn't know how to wear clothes. The expensive suit jacket did not fit, and his tie had slipped out of position.

Just then the swindler put a piece of paper on the desk next to the telegraph operator. *I'd like to know what that paper says,* Libby thought as the operator began tapping. For a moment he stopped, glancing up at the swindler, as though making sure he sent the right message.

A flicker of impatience crossed the swindler's face. Reaching forward, he pointed to the paper.

Something about his look nudged Libby's memory. *He's impatient,* Libby thought. But that wasn't what she needed to remember. What was it?

Then one word flicked into her mind. *Anger. How would that man look if he were angry?* Libby studied his face. He was clean-shaven and wore a hat. What if his face were red with anger?

Libby gasped. In that moment she knew who she was seeing. The man who robbed Pa's safe! The man who stole from Jordan's church and from Pa were one and the same person. *Edward Dexter!*

Libby tugged on Peter's arm, then signed Caleb's name. When Peter didn't want to leave, Libby insisted that they stay together. "Pa told me I'm supposed to take care of you," she wrote with three exclamation marks after her words. "Pa said we need to get help from a policeman or sheriff—someone like that."

Half running, half walking, Libby and Peter hurried back to the river for Caleb. By the time they again climbed the steep hill, Edward Dexter was gone.

"It's not your fault, Libby," Caleb said when he saw the disappointment in her face. "No swindler is going to stay around waiting for you to catch him."

"But I'm sure he was the man who robbed Pa. And Peter thinks he's the swindler who stole from Jordan."

To find the man this soon was better than they had hoped for.

But it also helped to be sure they were looking for one man, not two.

"Maybe he went to the address Serena found," Libby said. "If we go there, we'll find him again."

"Maybe." Caleb lowered his voice. "But I need to get back to Jordan. It's too dangerous for him where he is. In another hour or so, the riverfront will be empty unless a steamboat comes in. When the time is right, we'll go through a tunnel and find someone with the Underground Railroad. Jordan needs a better hiding place than a pile of wood anyone can search. If I say 'Run!' do what I do."

As they returned to the waterfront, the setting sun cast long shadows across the river into the town. Stopping along the side of the street, Libby took the slate from Peter and explained. But Peter didn't want to take the time needed to write a message. Instead he taught Libby and Caleb the sign for *Run away from someone!* Holding out his left hand, he swished his right hand against it with a swift upward motion.

Setting out again, Caleb led them back to the wharf. A steamboat was leaving now, and Caleb walked slowly, as though watching it turn into the current. While the shadows lengthened, he and Libby and Peter walked up and down, acting as if everything along the river was of interest to them.

In the dusk that followed the setting of the sun, Caleb nodded toward a steep rock wall at the edge of the waterfront. "Take a walk, Libby. You and Peter."

At first she wondered why Caleb sent her and Peter on. Then, as she drew closer to the steep hillside, she saw a crease in the land with a stream running down over the rock.

Not far from where the stream found its way to the river, Libby noticed a young pine tree, and near that, a small garden. In spite of the failing light, she saw hollyhocks rising tall and lovely next to the rock hillside.

A part of Libby felt pleased that someone had taken the time to plant flowers that close to a busy wharf and the railroad tracks that ran along the river. At the same time it made Libby curious.

Turning, she looked back to where Caleb leaned against a pile of wood.

Just then Libby caught a movement—Jordan standing up. Together he and Caleb crossed the tracks and soon reached Libby and Peter.

Going beyond them, Caleb hurried around the small pine tree. There he opened a door in the side of the rock wall. "Hurry," he whispered.

As Jordan slipped past Caleb into the darkness, Libby and Peter followed. Behind them, Libby heard the closing of a door, then Peter's gasp.

10

The Deserted House

"Where are we?" Libby's voice echoed against rock walls.

"Shhh!" Caleb warned, and Libby heard the sound of scratching. Then the flame of a candle glowed. But it was Peter who held the candle, not Caleb, as Libby expected.

The moment her gaze met his, Peter looked guilty. The bag on his back was still open, as though he had carried the candle and matches there.

So! Libby thought. *He still has a candle and matches. Just wait till I tell Pa!*

As though reading Libby's thoughts in her face, Peter's head shot up. "I'm not on the boat!"

That's true, Libby thought and didn't know what to do.

Already Caleb was lighting more candles. A small shelf near the door held a supply of them, as well as matches. As Caleb handed her one, Libby held it up. They were in a tunnel lined with brick. A steep stairway led upward, disappearing into the darkness.

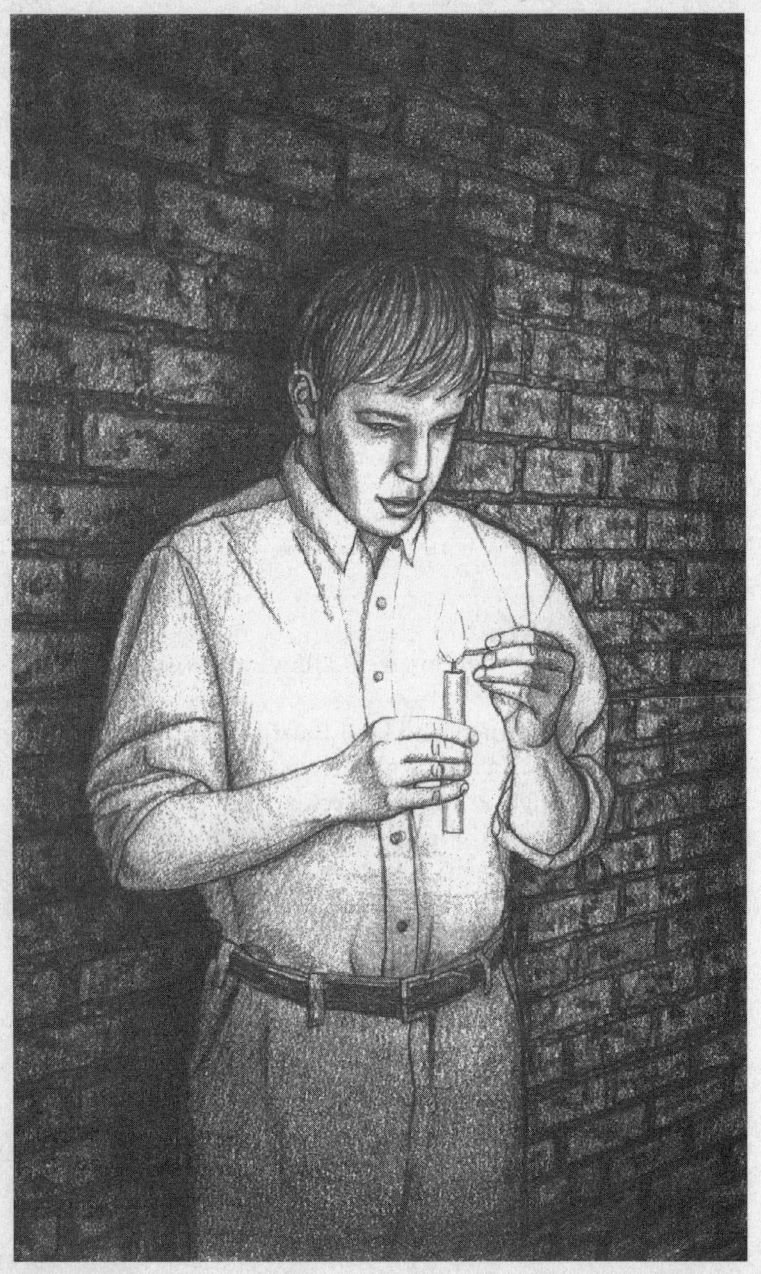

"Go ahead," Caleb said, his voice still a whisper. "You'll find a well partway up."

"A *well*?" Libby whispered back. "Caleb, how do you find these strange places?"

In the flickering light, Libby saw his grin and felt his relief that Jordan was in a safer place. "A man told me about this tunnel," Caleb said. "He also said there's an Underground Railroad station called the Rock House."

As Jordan started up the stairs, Peter grabbed a hand railing on the wall next to the steps. With Libby and Caleb following, they climbed stairs until the tunnel widened. Off to one side was the kind of three-foot-high round brick wall that surrounded a well. From a strong wooden beam above the well hung a rope with a pail.

"Spring-fed," Caleb said as they all stopped for a drink. "It's part of the town's water supply."

Walking on, they continued climbing for what must have been at least two or three blocks. More than once Libby stopped to rest and catch her breath. It seemed she had been climbing forever. Then she remembered the steep hills she had seen from the boat.

Still clutching his candle, Peter grabbed a railing each time they started out again. Where there was no railing, he caught hold of Libby's elbow and followed close behind.

Is he afraid of the dark? Libby wondered when he wavered as he walked. It didn't seem like Peter.

At last they came out in what looked like a cellar. Here, too, a small shelf was built into the brick to hold a supply of candles.

"What do we do now?" Jordan asked.

"I don't know," Caleb said. "I thought there would be someone here to meet us."

"Do you suppose this house is an Underground Railroad station?" Libby asked. Along the way she had noticed more than one door, as if different families used the tunnel to go for water.

"I'm sure it's a cellar," Caleb said. "But I don't know who lives here. The man who told me about the Rock House said it was a couple miles up from the river. We can't possibly have come that far."

Just then Libby heard a sound, as if someone walked above them. Holding up her candle, she saw the wooden beams of a floor.

"What if the wrong person finds us?" Libby whispered, feeling more creepy by the minute. In the candlelight Peter's eyes were wide, as if he wasn't sure that he liked what was happening.

"I am starting to feel like a mouse in a trap," Jordan said. "If this is the Underground Railroad, I want to make sure whose train I am on."

"Caleb, is there some signal you're supposed to give?" Libby asked.

"If there is, I don't know it."

By now Jordan was exploring. A short flight of steps, different from the one they had been on, led upward. At the top was a wooden door. Jordan blew out his candle, then opened the door a crack. Cool night air swept in.

While the rest of them waited at the bottom of the steps, Jordan took a peek outside. "Tell you what," he whispered as he closed the door again. "I am going to walk out on the street and let some Underground Railroad conductor find me."

"Look confused," Caleb said. "That's how I spot someone who needs help."

Jordan grinned. "That won't be hard. But I have a sneaking idea what might happen."

"If there's a Railroad conductor around, he'll talk to you," Caleb said, as though trying to sound hopeful. "If there's a slave catcher—"

Caleb didn't have to finish.

"Oh, Caleb, don't tease," Libby said. "Purposely set yourself up to be found by a slave catcher?" They could be headed into big trouble.

"Should we run?" Peter asked.

Libby signed back. "I don't know."

But Jordan wasn't going to wait for Libby to make up her mind. Without another word he opened the door, slipped out, and quietly closed the door behind him.

As Libby, Caleb, and Peter waited for what seemed forever, the floorboards above them creaked again.

What if the wrong person comes down in the cellar? Libby wondered again.

In the flickering light, tall shadows leaped up, seeming to surround them. Then a mouse ran across the floor and under the bottom step. Libby gulped and backed away.

"Are you scared, Libby?" Peter asked.

Libby felt ashamed. Pa had told her to be responsible for Peter. Right now she felt as if he was taking care of her.

Then quietly, on oiled hinges, the door to the outside opened.

"C'mon!" Jordan whispered.

"Ahhh!" Libby breathed deep with relief. Jordan must have found a man from the Underground Railroad.

But when Libby hurried outside, a fairly small, light-skinned woman stood there.

"Put out your candle," she whispered, and Libby obeyed, embarrassed that she had forgotten.

"Follow me."

Soon Libby lost track of the streets and the direction. She only knew that the woman moved quickly, wasting no time in bringing them into a frame clapboard church. When she closed the door behind them, she pushed aside a heavy curtain enough to let in a sliver of moonlight. Then she asked, "Why are you here?"

"These are my friends," Jordan said quickly. "I am looking for my daddy."

"You think he's taken the Underground Railroad?"

"If he's gotten this far." Jordan explained what had happened. "I think my daddy swam across the river. I want to find him—to tell him where our family is."

"You came to just the right person."

"Is this your church?" Libby asked.

"It is the Lord's church," the woman answered.

"Where are we?" Libby asked.

"The Alton AME Church. African Methodist Episcopal. My name is Priscilla Baltimore."

"Miz Priscilla," Jordan asked. "Is there some way to find out if my daddy made it this far?"

"I'll ask around," the woman told him. "If I don't hear anything, he might have crossed the river farther up. Tell me where he started from."

When Jordan finished his story, Miss Priscilla said, "I can't make the trip tonight. If I need to find out more, I'll row across the river tomorrow night."

"Do you want me to go with you and help you row?" Caleb asked quickly.

"Thank you kindly," she answered. "But if I go by myself, I'll have an empty boat for bringing back any runaways I find."

In the dark Libby wished she could see Caleb's expression. Clearly Priscilla Baltimore was a woman who did not sit home waiting for fugitives to come to her. She went out and found them.

"I'll bring food before I take you farther on," she said.

Libby had no idea how hungry she was until Miss Priscilla returned with a kettle of soup. To Libby's amazement she dished it up with only the one sliver of light from where the curtain was pushed slightly aside.

While they finished eating, Priscilla Baltimore talked to Jordan. "I'll take you to the Rock House. You'll be safe there till I learn something about your daddy."

When Miss Priscilla returned for Libby, Caleb, and Peter, she told them, "We're hiding a lot of people right now. Since no one is looking for you, you can stay at Major Hunter's. They have a lodging place where you can get food and sleep."

"We're also looking for a swindler," Caleb said. "We have an address that might help us find him. Can you tell us where it is?"

On the way to Major Hunter's, Miss Priscilla brought them to the address on the piece of paper Serena had found. Now, in the middle of the night, the house looked deserted, as if no one had lived there for some time. Libby and Caleb decided to come back the next day.

In the light of the moon, Miss Priscilla led them on through the empty streets. At last she stopped outside the lodging place. Far above, against the night sky, was the outline of two chimneys—one on either end of the house.

When Miss Priscilla rapped a special knock, the door quietly opened. Major Hunter's wife, Rebecca, stood in the dark, ready to welcome them. Though Miss Priscilla didn't say so, Libby felt sure that Major and Mrs. Hunter were leaders in the Underground Railroad.

That night Libby had a small room all to herself and sank down into a soft bed. Yet her last waking thought was about runaway slaves who walked all night, then slept in whatever place they could find. In order to reach freedom, how many of them were cold and hungry and afraid at this very moment? When the sun came up, how many fugitives would sleep in the woods or in a wet, snake-filled swamp?

In the morning Rebecca Hunter served Libby, Caleb, and Peter a big breakfast with eggs and ham and thick slices of bread. While they were eating, Libby heard the *chink, chink, chink* of a hammer striking a chisel.

"What's going on?" she asked.

Mrs. Hunter smiled. "Our friend John Livingston asked a man to check our chimneys. Reverend Livingston used to run the press for another friend of ours, Elijah Lovejoy."

"Mr. Lovejoy was your friend?" Caleb asked, as though hardly daring to believe what he'd heard.

Mrs. Hunter nodded, a shadow of sadness in her eyes.

"Will you tell me about him?" Caleb asked. Some time before, he had told Libby that a mob killed Elijah Lovejoy at Alton, then threw his fourth printing press into the river.

"Elijah was a teacher, writer, newspaper editor," Mrs. Hunter said. "A Presbyterian minister, a man of God. Do you know all that?"

Caleb nodded. "Elijah Lovejoy is my hero."

"Then you want to know what he said and wrote. I have extra

copies of his most famous words. Would you like to take them along when you leave?"

Caleb's face shone as though unable to believe such a great gift.

"But now, while you're here, let me tell you some of the words I remember." Mrs. Hunter cleared her throat, as though wanting to be sure she gave the words the way Elijah Lovejoy did.

Then she began: " 'As long as I am an American citizen, and as long as American blood runs in these veins, I shall hold myself at liberty to speak, to write, to publish whatever I please on any subject I please, being amenable to the laws of my country for the same.' "

On the slate Libby explained to Peter, "Mr. Lovejoy wanted to write and publish with freedom. But he also wanted to respect the laws of our country."

For a moment Caleb was silent. Then, as though thinking aloud, he summed up Mr. Lovejoy's words. "He wanted to speak, write, and publish what he believed needed to be said? That's freedom of the press. But he didn't want to say just whatever he felt like, even if it hurt people? He wanted to be responsible about what he wrote?"

Mrs. Hunter nodded. "He respected a higher law—God's law. Elijah believed that God has taught us to care about the worth of every human being."

"He didn't change his mind when things got hard?" Caleb asked.

Mrs. Hunter shook her head. "He never stopped working for what he believed was right."

Again Caleb was silent. Finally he asked, "Is Elijah Lovejoy the first American to die for freedom of the press?"

"As far as I know," Mrs. Hunter answered. "But Elijah died not only for freedom of the press. He died for the freedom of our colored friends. I remember something else he said. 'I have sworn eternal opposition to slavery, and by the blessing of God I will never turn back.' "

Mrs. Hunter stood up to offer more food. "You know, Caleb,

you should meet Reverend Livingston. He's been a pastor here in Alton, and he's known as the father of the Colored Baptists in Illinois. He's coming to see my husband this afternoon. If you're here at three o'clock, you could talk to Reverend Livingston first."

"We'll go now," Caleb answered, as if suddenly remembering they were supposed to be searching for the swindler. "But we'll do our best to be back in time."

Soon Libby, Caleb, and Peter reached the house at the address Miss Priscilla had shown them. Set a short distance away from any other home, it was built on the side of a steep hill. In the daylight the house seemed even more deserted.

After looking around, Libby and the boys found a hiding place behind some bushes. There they had a good view of both the house and the hill leading up to it. The three of them settled down to watch for the swindler.

By the end of the first hour, Caleb was restless. When a second hour passed, he could no longer sit still. Standing up, he started to prowl around the area.

"Stop it, Caleb!" Libby said. "You'll give us away."

When Caleb sat down again, Peter began teaching them the finger alphabet. Then he said, "We should have our own secret sign for *danger ahead*." Peter showed them how to make a *D*, then an *A*.

Peter's many abilities made Libby curious. "Where did you learn to sign?" she asked on Peter's slate.

"At the Illinois Institution for the Education of the Deaf and Dumb," he said.

"In Jacksonville?" Caleb wrote.

Peter nodded. "During school that's where I live. That's where I learned to talk with my hands. All my friends are there."

Caleb leaned forward. "We want to be your friends too," he wrote.

A grin lit Peter's face, reaching even his eyes. "You are," he said.

It was past two o'clock when Caleb started his restless prowling again. "We have wasted a good part of the day just sitting around!"

Libby felt disappointed, but she had to agree. At the same time, she wondered what to do about it. "We don't have any other leads for the swindler. Where can he be?"

"You think you saw him at the train station—" Caleb began.

"We *know* we saw him," Libby answered. "Peter is sure it was the man he saw walking toward the boardinghouse. I'm sure it was the swindler who tried to cheat the immigrant on the *Christina*."

By now Caleb was more impatient than Libby had ever seen him. He was used to doing things, not sitting around. "I want to talk to Reverend Livingston," he said. "If we stay any longer, we'll miss him."

When Caleb explained to Peter, the boy said, "I'll stay and watch for the swindler."

"Alone?" Libby wrote. She wasn't sure about that. Pa had told her to be responsible for Peter.

"I've taken care of myself a long time," Peter said. "You don't have to treat me like a baby."

Libby felt the warm flush of embarrassment reach her cheeks. That's what she had been doing, all right. But now she wrote, "You promise to hide from the swindler if he comes?"

"I'll find you," Peter said. "If the swindler doesn't come by sundown, I'll go to Hunter's just before dark."

With that agreement, Caleb and Libby left. She understood Peter wanting to be on his own. She *had* been treating him like a baby. But halfway back to Hunter's, Libby started thinking it over.

"Caleb, did we do the right thing?" she asked. "Leaving Peter, I mean?"

"Aw, Libby, stop acting like an old mother hen! You heard what Peter told you."

Again Libby felt embarrassed. But she could not shake off her uneasiness.

11

Caleb's Hero

Soon after Libby and Caleb reached Major Hunter's lodging place, Reverend John Livingston arrived. When Libby saw the lines of kindness in his face, she knew this father of the Colored Baptist churches in Illinois was a man to be trusted.

When Caleb explained what he wanted to know, Reverend Livingston listened carefully.

"Elijah Lovejoy was my friend," he said. "Sometimes I could almost hear the Lord saying, 'John, I am giving you the privilege of running this man's press. I am giving you the privilege of printing what he says.' "

Reverend Livingston led them into the backyard and to a bench where they could sit down and talk.

"What do you remember most about Mr. Lovejoy?" Caleb asked.

"The kind of person he was. My white brother died because he cared about people like me. Even now, after twenty years, I can't forget some of the things he wrote. I especially remember him saying, 'The fittest place for man to die is where he dies for man.' "

Reverend Livingston's eyes were wet. "Elijah Lovejoy knew Jesus, and Jesus died for every one of us who has ever been a slave."

Leaning forward, Reverend Livingston looked directly into Caleb's face. "Mrs. Hunter told me that Elijah Lovejoy is your hero. What do you plan to do about that?"

Caleb stared at him, startled.

When he did not answer, Libby wanted to jump in, to tell the minister about Caleb's work with the Underground Railroad. But Caleb made no mention of that.

As the silence grew long, Libby's thoughts raced on. *I could tell Reverend Livingston how brave Caleb is.* Just in time she realized that would make him uncomfortable.

Then Caleb looked into the minister's eyes. As though Libby were no longer there, he spoke. "I want to be a man of honor—to do what's right, even though no one knows about it. I want to do what I know to be true, even when there's no reward in doing it."

"Ah!" Reverend Livingston leaned back, smiling as though he had received a better answer than he could have hoped for. "Then, Caleb, I will pray for you every day."

When they stood up to leave, Caleb had one more question. "Do you know where Elijah Lovejoy is buried?"

"There is one man who might know." Then Reverend Livingston shook his head. "If he does know, he won't tell you. But why don't you talk to a newspaperman named Thomas Dimmock? I'll give you directions to his house."

As Libby and Caleb started away, John Livingston spoke again. "If you follow Jordan's daddy up the state of Illinois, you might go to Jacksonville or Springfield. If you ever need a place of refuge—" The minister was looking at Caleb, but Libby knew what he was saying.

When Libby and Caleb reached the address Reverend Livingston had given them, a man with a full mustache and a well-trimmed beard opened the door.

"Mr. Dimmock?" Caleb asked. "Reverend Livingston gave us your name. Can you tell us how to find Elijah Lovejoy's grave?"

When Mr. Dimmock glanced back into the parlor, Libby saw a group of men gathered there. Shutting the door behind him, Mr. Dimmock looked up and down the street, then led Libby and Caleb away from the parlor windows.

"Who are you?" Mr. Dimmock asked.

"A cabin boy on the *Christina*," Caleb answered. "This is Libby Norstad. Her pa is the captain."

Mr. Dimmock offered a warm smile to Libby. "I know your father. He's a good man, a fair man."

He turned back to Caleb. "Why do you want to see Elijah Lovejoy's grave?"

"He's my hero," Caleb said simply.

"Why is he your hero?" Mr. Dimmock sounded curious now.

"He was a newspaper man. A writer and editor like I want to be. He stood for the things I want to stand for."

Listening to Caleb, Libby suddenly felt uncomfortable. She couldn't help but admire him, but deep down she felt scared. How could Caleb say things like that? There was a cost to standing for the right things, a cost Mr. Lovejoy had known well.

Now Caleb's face was slightly flushed, as though he found it hard to talk this way to a stranger. Yet he looked at the man without wavering. "I don't know if I can do it, but I want to stand for the things I believe in."

"I see," Mr. Dimmock answered, his gaze still holding Caleb's. "Elijah Lovejoy's grave is not marked. I suspect there's just one man who knows exactly where it is. I can only tell you approximately where it might be. You understand there won't be anything to see?"

Caleb nodded.

"If I take you there, will you and Libby make me a solemn promise?"

"That we don't tell anyone where you think the grave might be?" Caleb answered.

Mr. Dimmock nodded.

"We promise," Caleb said instantly.

But Mr. Dimmock wasn't satisfied with that. "You too?" he asked Libby.

"Me too." Libby's voice was solemn.

"You understand the danger of telling even one person?" Again Mr. Dimmock searched their faces.

"We understand that someone might be disrespectful to his grave," Caleb answered.

Finally Mr. Dimmock nodded, as if satisfied that he could trust them. "When I was seven years old, I lived across the street from the cemetery. I knew that Mr. Lovejoy had been killed by a mob. I saw his friends come to the cemetery."

Again Mr. Dimmock glanced around, as though making sure that no one could hear. "Can you meet me at the cemetery half an hour before sunset?"

When Caleb agreed, he spoke quickly. "One more thing. We have a friend who's a runaway slave. Can we bring him too?"

"A runaway slave?" A quiet smile lit Mr. Dimmock's face. "That's the kind of person Mr. Lovejoy died for. I think he would like to have a fugitive visit his grave."

As the sun slanted down toward the western horizon, Libby and Caleb walked to the Rock House, where Jordan was hiding.

"I heard people talking about Miz Priscilla today," Jordan said the minute he saw them. "Did you know she rows the bishop of the AME Church across the river? And she gathers up slaves for church meetings."

Jordan grinned. "Once slave owners in Missouri let her take three hundred slaves to Illinois so they could hear preaching about Jesus."

That afternoon Priscilla Baltimore had stopped to ask Jordan more questions about his daddy. At sundown she would cross the Mississippi to search for Micah Parker.

"Miz Priscilla said that if we left here we should walk as if we belong together," Jordan told Caleb as they headed toward the cemetery. "We should walk as if you're saying I belong to you. I am all right."

Half an hour before sunset the three of them entered the cemetery. As they walked slowly around, Jordan tried to read the gravestones. Caleb helped him sound out the easier names and words.

Within a few minutes, Mr. Dimmock strolled across the street and stopped at a stone near the entrance. Soon he moved on.

Passing close to Caleb, he spoke in a low voice. "Follow me."

A short distance away, Mr. Dimmock stopped. Turning, he faced a road that ran from the entrance of the cemetery to an area farther back. Gravestones stood on either side of the road.

When Caleb, then Libby and Jordan, turned to face the same direction, Mr. Dimmock spoke quietly. "I believe the grave is somewhere beneath that road."

As Libby stared at the dirt path, tears welled up in her eyes. *No marker, not even a cross.* Though Mr. Dimmock had warned them, she felt upset.

Then he spoke again. "The time will come when we can mark Mr. Lovejoy's grave. But first we will have war—civil war. Neighbor will fight against neighbor and brother against brother."

War? Libby dreaded even the sound of the word.

For a time all of them stood without speaking. Then, as Libby glanced sideways, she saw Caleb's face. It was all he could do to keep from breaking down. A hurt look filled his eyes—a look of grieving for a hero he could never meet in person.

As though Thomas Dimmock sensed what Caleb was thinking, he spoke quietly. "Someday the world will know that Elijah Lovejoy died for the freedom of slaves. Someday there will be a monument here—a monument that honors the first American martyr for freedom of the press."

As Libby blinked away her tears, Jordan bowed his head. His

lips moved, but no sound came, and Libby knew he was praying.

When at last he looked up, Jordan stood tall. Though his gaze still rested on a spot in the road, his eyes shone with pride.

Then Caleb straightened his shoulders, as if he had decided something. Finally he spoke. "A good road goes somewhere."

"Yes," Mr. Dimmock answered. "A good road helps all of us."

"I want to make sure I'm on the right one," Caleb said.

With darkness falling around them, Libby and Caleb walked with Jordan back to the Rock House. On the long return trip to Major Hunter's, Libby thought about all she had seen and heard.

It had been their search for stolen money that started all this—money taken from Pa and from Jordan's church. But now Libby had only one thought. *Money doesn't seem very important compared to Elijah Lovejoy's life.*

When they reached the lodging place, Mrs. Hunter met them at the door. "I saved dinner for you because I thought you'd be late."

"Peter?" Libby asked, suddenly remembering. "Is he here?"

When Mrs. Hunter told them no, Libby's heart lurched with fear. "It's dark, and Peter hasn't come back," she said to Caleb. "I told you we shouldn't leave him alone."

By now they had discovered a shortcut—a more direct way to cross the hill to what they called the swindler's house. As Caleb and Libby hurried through the streets, her dread grew with the darkness.

"Pa told me to look out for Peter," she said. "I'm sure not doing a good job of it."

Caleb tried to calm her down. "Just wait till you see what's happened to Peter."

But Libby was growing frantic. "What if the swindler found him and knew that Peter could identify him?"

Even Caleb had no answer for that.

When they reached the swindler's house, nothing seemed to have changed. Curtains still covered the windows. Weeds filled the flower gardens. No candle or lamplight glowed from within. Libby and Caleb walked straight to where they had hidden twice before. Peter was nowhere. When they circled the house, there was not one trace of him. Clouds had covered the sky and whatever light there was.

"I can't believe I did this to Peter," Libby said. "I can't believe I went off and left him on his own."

"He's used to being on his own. He even told you to stop treating him like a baby."

"But where is he?" Libby's voice broke. "I'm scared, Caleb. Really scared!" Filled with panic, Libby couldn't begin to think what to try next.

12

Narrow Escape

Through long practice in working with the Underground Railroad, Caleb had learned to hide his feelings. Yet he looked upset as he walked over to the edge of the yard. Below where Caleb stood, the ground dropped sharply away in the steep wooded hills of Alton.

When Libby came to stand beside him, she saw lightning bugs blink their lights. On that last night of July, the yellow lights flashed here, then there. Libby had always liked to watch lightning bugs, but now she was in no mood to enjoy them.

Farther away, lamps glowed from the windows of homes. Then Libby noticed another kind of light on a street below them. The light bobbed around, and at first Libby wondered if she was seeing more lightning bugs. Then she decided, *No. The light moves strangely, but it doesn't go out. Someone is holding a candle.*

"Caleb," Libby said. "See that light down there? It looks like someone is weaving around." She could think of no other explanation for the way the light moved back and forth.

"Whoever it is, he's walking in a zigzag," Caleb answered. "If it's a man who would scare Peter—"

In that moment Caleb made up his mind. "There's no one here at the house. Let's see if Peter took that way back to Hunter's."

Walking fast, Libby and Caleb hurried down the steep hill. Whenever they lost sight of the strangely moving light, they began to run.

As they started to catch up, Libby realized that whoever held the candle had to be quite short. Then, against the dark night, she saw a darker outline of the person.

"It's Peter with a lighted candle!" Libby exclaimed. Though relieved to find him, Libby felt angry. "There is he, disobeying again."

"But he's not on the *Christina,*" Caleb pointed out. "Let's not scare him. He can't hear us coming. We shouldn't jump out at him from the dark."

Breaking into a run, Caleb left the road to circle around Peter, then came out where the boy could see him. Soon after Caleb and Peter met, Libby caught up with them.

Taking the slate, Caleb began writing. "Is something wrong?"

Clearly puzzled, Peter shook his head. "A man came up the street," he said. "I waited to see if it was the swindler. By the time I could leave, it was dark."

"Are you all right?" Caleb wrote.

"Can't you see me?" Peter asked. "Of course I am!"

Caleb looked at Libby, as though not sure what to do. But Peter solved the problem for them. Realizing that Libby was worried, he held up his candle.

"I had brain fever when I was seven years old. My parents had it too. That's how they died. And that's why I'm deaf."

Peter spoke quietly, as if he still didn't want to tell them what was wrong. "I have trouble with my balance in the dark. Even with a candle, I can't walk straight."

Early the next morning, Libby, Caleb, and Peter were eating breakfast with Mrs. Hunter when Priscilla Baltimore came to the door. She stepped inside carrying a laundry basket. Libby wondered if she really did do laundry or if it was a way of hiding her work with the Underground Railroad. Then she began lifting carefully ironed laundry from her basket.

Though probably in her late fifties, Miss Priscilla moved with the energy of a young girl. "I've already talked to Jordan," she said. "The slave catchers aren't sure if his father drowned or if he managed to swim the Mississippi. They're searching this side of the river now."

"Do you think Micah Parker is in Alton?" Caleb asked.

"If he is, none of the conductors I know have seen him."

Caleb groaned.

"But—" Miss Priscilla held up her hand. "There's a place north of Alton you can try. The Monticello Seminary, a school for girls in Godfrey. It's the kind of place Jordan's daddy might find on his own."

Caleb stood up. "Let's go," he said to Libby and Peter. Then he turned to the two women. "What should we do to hide Jordan?"

"All our wagons and buggies will be in use," Mrs. Hunter answered.

"The town is swarming with slave catchers," Miss Priscilla added. "It's a dangerous time for any colored person, whether a runaway or free."

"Jordan doesn't have a pass," Caleb told her. "And he doesn't have papers saying that he's free."

"Most catchers know that documents like that are forged," she said. "You will have to be Jordan's pass, his freedom papers. Walk down the street as if it's all right that Jordan walks with you."

There it is again, Libby thought. *Already Miss Priscilla had told Jordan the same thing. Walk as if you belong to Caleb.*

"How far is it to the school for girls?" Caleb asked.

"Take a stagecoach," Miss Priscilla told him. "It will give Jordan a better hiding place."

"When should we go?"

"If you wait for the morning train to come in from St. Louis, there will be plenty of stages near the station. But don't go yet. There would be too much time for Jordan to be seen."

When Miss Priscilla left, Libby and Caleb talked about what to do. Peter offered a reminder. "We haven't found the swindler."

Using the few signs he had learned from Peter, Caleb half signed, half wrote, "Libby and I will go to the swindler's house. You go to the Rock House. Tell Jordan we'll come there for both of you."

"We need to catch the swindler in the act of doing something wrong," Caleb said as he and Libby walked to the deserted house.

"Or prove that he has the money stolen from Pa and from Jordan?" asked Libby.

"That would do it." Caleb sounded as if he wanted to make sure they could put everything together. "I like Peter's secret sign for danger ahead. But we need another signal, too—a way of knocking so we know who is there."

"A secret knock, you mean?" Libby's throat felt dry. What was going to happen that Caleb felt they needed that?

"How about this?" Caleb rapped against his fist in three even knocks. "That means *It's me, Caleb.*"

"And I rap back?" Libby tried it, using a different pattern. *Long, short, long.*

When Caleb and Libby reached the swindler's house, they knew something had changed during the night. One of the curtains was in a slightly different position.

Kneeling down behind the bushes, they waited, but not for long. The man Libby knew as Edward Dexter came out, then closed and locked the front door. In each hand he carried a cloth bag with handles. As he started down the hill, Libby and Caleb followed at a safe distance.

After all the waiting, Libby felt excited but frightened too. "What if we see him do something wrong?" she whispered.

"Find a policeman," Caleb answered.

As they hurried down the hill, Libby watched for a policeman. Edward Dexter headed straight for the ticket window at the train depot. Doing his best not to be seen by the swindler, Caleb edged close.

When he returned to Libby, they slipped behind a freight wagon to decide what to do.

"Where is Dexter going?" Libby asked.

"Brighton. It's north of Alton on the way to Springfield. Dexter is leaving on the morning train. That means I've got only two hours to get Jordan and Peter."

Caleb began pulling coins from his pockets. "Do you have money?"

"Not much." Libby took out what she had. When she left the *Christina,* she didn't want to ask Pa for money with the deadline for the loan on August fifteenth. *Today is Saturday, August first,* Libby thought with dread. *The loan is due two weeks from today.*

Near the train station, several stagecoach drivers waited, ready to pick up passengers.

"Find out if there's a stage going to Monticello Seminary," Caleb said.

"We're not going to Brighton?"

"We have to choose." Already Caleb had made up his mind. "We'll look for Jordan's father in Godfrey, then go to Brighton."

Caleb grinned, as if glad to be doing something again. "I need to run. While I get Jordan and Peter, you buy us tickets."

On one side of the depot, three stagecoach drivers waited. When Libby found one who was driving past the school for girls, she bought four tickets. "My friends will be coming," she told the driver.

As Libby waited, each minute seemed to stretch into hours. *How far is the Rock House?* she wondered, then decided it must be about two miles from the riverfront. But she had learned one thing in Alton. Walking up the steep hills always took longer than she expected. Libby's leg muscles felt sore just thinking about the climb.

Growing more and more nervous, Libby kept watching all

TICKETS

around her. Then, from far away on the downstream side of Alton, Libby heard a train whistle. Long and lonely it sounded, and it reminded Libby of how she missed Pa. In that moment she remembered they had promised to leave a message for him.

Quickly Libby stepped into the depot and scribbled a note about where they were headed. Here, too, the swindler was nowhere in sight, but Libby knew he could be in the waiting room set aside for men.

Soon after she returned to the stagecoach, Libby heard a closer whistle. A few minutes later, she saw the engine, then heard the clank of cars coming to a stop next to the station. As workers began unloading baggage, Caleb, Jordan, and Peter hurried up to Libby.

With relief, she gave the stagecoach tickets to Caleb. Opening the door of the stage, Caleb pushed Jordan toward one of the seats. But the driver stopped them.

"Coloreds on the top," he said.

Caleb turned to him. "He's traveling with me."

"Are you his owner?" the driver asked.

Caleb opened his mouth, but no words came. For an instant he stood there, as if trying to think of a way to answer without lying.

"Are you his owner?" the driver asked again.

Unwilling to lie, Caleb straightened. "No, sir, I'm not. I don't believe in owning anyone."

Libby gulped. Caleb was going to start a scene right there.

"Then your friend has to go on top of the stage."

An angry flush crept into Caleb's face. Libby tugged his sleeve, trying to warn him to stop. But suddenly Jordan stepped forward.

"Caleb, I like the view from the top."

Already Jordan was scrambling up. Quickly settling himself between the carpetbags, he turned so that his face was hidden from anyone at the depot.

Caleb had no choice but to follow Libby and Peter onto the stage. When the three of them sat down on one of the red cushioned seats, Caleb exploded. "Someday this is going to change!"

Libby agreed, but before Jordan's quick decision to ride on top, she had seen him looking around. For some reason he wanted to leave in a hurry. Why?

With Peter sitting on one side and Caleb on the other, Libby leaned forward to look out a window. There, on the platform next to the train station, was the man Libby had hoped she would never see again. Jordan's owner, the slavetrader, Riggs!

As a large gentleman boarded the stage, Libby whispered in Caleb's ear. "Jordan knew we needed to leave." She tipped her head toward the window.

When the gentleman sat down opposite Libby, she tapped the bag for Peter's slate. When he took it out, she wrote quickly, then held it so only Caleb and Peter could see: RIGGS!

Standing up, Caleb tried to see out the window on Peter's side. Finally he shrugged his shoulders as if to ask, "Where?"

Again Libby peered out the window. "He's gone," she wrote. "Maybe he got on the train."

Caleb shook his head, then spoke softly instead of writing. "That train just came from St. Louis," he reminded her. "Unless—"

"Unless he took a breath of fresh air and went back on. Is that the train for Brighton?" Libby asked.

"Godfrey, then Brighton, then up the state of Illinois to Springfield and Chicago."

His eyes wide, Peter poked Libby. "What's going on?"

Writing quickly, Libby explained that Riggs was the man from whom Jordan ran away. Still writing, she asked Caleb, "Do you think Riggs knows something we don't?"

"I wonder why he came from St. Louis right now." This time Caleb remembered to write so that Peter understood.

"Maybe it's just a coincidence," Libby answered.

"I wish I could believe that, but I can't."

Libby's stomach tightened with nervousness. "You think that Riggs knows Jordan is in the area?"

"Remember what Riggs said the first time we saw him?"

Caleb wrote. "That no slave ever got away from him alive. Maybe Riggs has a special hatred for Jordan because he *did* manage to get away."

"Or else he knows Jordan's father." Tugging at a strand of hair, Libby nervously twisted it around her finger. "Maybe Riggs knows that Micah Parker ran away too."

"Either way, we're in big trouble," Caleb said.

Just then a woman with two young children boarded the stagecoach. As they squeezed onto the seat next to the large gentleman, Libby thought, *Good! With the stagecoach full, the driver should leave.*

Again Peter poked her. Libby was only beginning to learn that he caught every expression in her eyes. Giving the secret sign for *danger ahead* and the letter *J* for Jordan, he raised his eyebrows. Libby knew Peter was asking a question.

Libby nodded.

Putting the palms of his hands together, Peter held them up, as if praying. In spite of her fear, Libby smiled. Where he had learned to pray, she didn't know, but she felt glad that Peter knew what to do.

When the driver called "Giddyup!" Libby drew a breath of relief. Yet she couldn't help wondering where they would see Riggs again.

13

Last Chance?

On the way to Monticello Seminary, Caleb told them why Benjamin Godfrey had started the school for girls. "One day he noticed how much his five daughters learned from their mother. He decided, 'I'm going to educate my girls because mothers teach the rulers of the world.' "

Caleb grinned at Libby. "So you see how important it is that you're smart?"

Libby made a face at him. "What if the swindler leaves Brighton before we get there?"

"If we need to take a train, do you have money?" Caleb asked.

"You know I don't."

"Mr. Godfrey was the managing contractor and builder for the St. Louis, Alton and Chicago Railroad. I'm going to ask him for railroad passes."

"He'll give you a pass, just like that?" Libby snapped her fingers.

"He and Elijah Lovejoy were friends. I suspect that Mr. Godfrey would like to see Micah Parker reach freedom."

When the driver stopped the stage, Libby climbed down and

stood in front of a building so tall that she counted the windows. Six stories high!

As the stage rattled off in a cloud of dust, Jordan walked boldly up to the entrance. When he knocked on the large oak door, a woman opened it partway. But she waited before inviting them inside.

Jordan quickly explained. "I am looking for my daddy. Me and Momma and my sisters and my brother need to find him."

"Do you know if he came this way?" the woman asked.

"We think he swam the river to get away from slave catchers." Jordan spoke quickly before the woman could shut the door. "Me and my friends forgot to ask the password. But I know Priscilla Baltimore." Jordan motioned toward the others. "They know Major Hunter and his wife."

Caleb stepped forward. "Mrs. Hunter told me to ask for Benjamin Godfrey."

Convinced now, the woman led them to the nearby Presbyterian church. Instead of passing under the tall pillars at the front of the beautiful white building, she took them around to a more hidden entrance. When Jordan and Peter disappeared inside, Caleb and Libby went on to Mr. Godfrey's house.

Mr. Godfrey listened to Caleb, then said, "There are five of you, counting Jordan's father? I'd be glad to give you passes. Then you can get on or off one of our trains whenever needed."

Sitting back in his chair, Mr. Godfrey rubbed his clean-shaven chin, as though thinking hard. "You're looking for *both* a swindler and a runaway slave? Sounds like you might need help somewhere along the way. Have you met the detective Allan Pinkerton?"

Libby and Caleb had only heard about him. While living in the little village of Dundee, Illinois, Mr. Pinkerton and his wife had become involved in the work of the Underground Railroad. At all hours of the day and night they opened their doors to help runaway slaves. After moving to Chicago, Mr. Pinkerton had started the Pinkerton Detective Agency.

"Keep on the lookout for him," Mr. Godfrey said. "He has an

Irish accent. That may help you find him. He's riding our trains now to stop any trouble that might come up."

When Libby and Caleb returned to the church, they found a number of runaway slaves, some of them with families, waiting until it was safe to go on. Jordan had been busy talking to church members who brought food and clothing for fugitives.

"No one has seen my daddy," Jordan said. "But I found out where to look next. In Brighton there's a man named Dr. Thomas Brown. His house is the main Underground Railroad station in town. Maybe we'll find Daddy and the swindler too."

As soon as it was dark, Underground Railroad conductors began coming to the room. The conductors led fugitives from one station, or safe place, to the next. Now and then they took a larger group in order to keep a family together. More often they led only a few fugitives at a time because it was easier to avoid being seen.

When the night wore on and no one came for them, Libby grew tired of waiting. "Can't we just go on by ourselves?" she asked.

But Caleb shook his head. Though he had been a conductor in northwestern Missouri and southeastern Iowa, he didn't know this area. "If it was just you and me and Peter, we could go alone," he explained. "But with Riggs around, I'm afraid what might happen to Jordan."

Finally Libby leaned back against a wall. When she fell asleep, she dreamed that she was back on the *Christina*. Tied up at a waterfront, the boat rocked gently, soothing Libby. But when she wakened, she felt confused about where she was.

Then she remembered. *It's Sunday.*

It made her lonesome for Pa. On Sunday morning he often stopped at a town to let the passengers and crew go to church. Other times Pa led worship services on board the *Christina*.

Now Libby wished that she could go to one of those services. It seemed hard to believe that a week had passed since she and Caleb and Peter visited Jordan's church.

Standing up, Libby stretched and tried to throw off the

weight she was feeling. *We're not doing too well,* she thought. *We can't find Jordan's father. We don't know how to catch the swindler.*

The more she thought about Edward Dexter, the more discouraged Libby felt. *The loan is due in only thirteen days. Will we ever find the money stolen from Pa? And how can we possibly clear Jordan's name?* Libby knew that Jordan would never feel satisfied until he proved he could be trusted.

At last an elderly man with thick white hair came for Jordan. Libby, Caleb, and Peter followed them out of the room. The Underground Railroad conductor led them toward a stairway. "Sit in different places around the church so it's not so obvious that you're strangers," he whispered as they started up. "At the end of the service, find me near the front door."

Libby and Peter stayed together, but the others scattered. *It's daylight,* Libby thought as she and Peter found a seat. *How is that conductor going to protect Jordan?*

During announcements Libby wrote a quick note on Peter's slate. When he learned the plan, he gave his sign for "All right! Yes! Yes!"

As soon as the congregation began singing, Libby's tiredness fell away. With each hymn they sang, she felt better, and she was glad they sang all the verses. But when the pastor started preaching, Libby wished she knew more sign language so she could tell Peter what he said. Then, to Libby's great amazement, the minister spoke on the verse Caleb had given her: "The Lord is my light and my salvation; whom shall I fear?"

"What is the pastor saying?" Peter whispered.

In that moment Libby felt good all over. So far, she could sign only a few words, but she knew the ones she needed. Turning, she faced Peter so he could see her hands and signed, "The Lord is my light."

Reaching into his pocket, Peter pulled out his candle. Holding it up, he grinned.

Libby smiled back, but it made her wonder. Did Peter have more than one reason for carrying a candle? Did the flame remind him of God's love for him?

When the service was over, Libby and Peter found Caleb, Jordan, and the Underground Railroad conductor waiting in the crowd by the door. With the elderly conductor leading them, they went through the line, shaking hands with the pastor.

Outside, the man took them to his two-seater buggy. In a low voice he spoke to Jordan. "There are slave catchers in the area. Pretend you usually drive us."

As though he was well acquainted with the horses, Jordan walked forward. Talking quietly to them, he untied their lead rope, then climbed up into the front seat. The Underground conductor sat next to Jordan, and Libby, Caleb, and Peter took the second seat.

Soon they fell into a long line of buggies and farm wagons returning home for Sunday dinner. Looking back, Libby gazed at the beautiful white church until the cross on its high steeple disappeared from sight.

Each time Jordan needed to make a turn, the white-haired conductor spoke in a low voice. Gradually the number of buggies and wagons grew less and less. As they traveled through a wooded area, the man gave them instructions. "I'm taking you to the Hill House, a stagecoach inn in Brighton," he said. "There will be a lot of people coming and going. You won't be so noticeable coming in there."

The conductor turned to Libby and the boys in the backseat. "When Jordan stops the horses, the rest of you go into the inn with me. When I sit down at a table, walk through the inn and out the back door, as if you want to use the outhouse. The Brighton train station is about two blocks away. The station for the *real* railroad, I mean. It would be a good place for all of you to meet."

"Where does Dr. Brown live?" Caleb asked.

"Three blocks beyond the railroad depot. There are woods across the street from his front door. You'll know you have the right house if you see a lantern sitting on a post in the backyard. If you have trouble, hide in the woods until someone lights the lantern. That's your signal that it's safe to knock on the door."

When they stepped down from the stagecoach at the Hill

House, Libby saw that the conductor had made a wise choice. At the front entrance, there was so much activity that no one seemed to notice a few more people.

Libby, Caleb, and Peter followed the conductor up the steps. As they entered a large dining room, Peter was the first one behind the man who was helping them. Suddenly Peter turned around. With his back to the room, he signed *Danger ahead!* then pointed toward one of the tables.

Uh-oh! Libby thought as she looked in that direction. *The swindler. Just exactly who we wanted to find. But not now, not yet. We need to watch him, not have him see us.*

Whirling around, Libby almost stumbled into Caleb. "Dexter!" she whispered.

She didn't think the swindler would recognize her, but what about Peter? He had seen the man in Galena, then in Alton. And what if Dexter looked through a window and saw Jordan?

As though she were still seeing him, Libby remembered how Dexter held up his clenched fist. "I'll get even with you!" he had told Pa. Could one of those ways of getting even be to make trouble for Jordan?

"What do we do?" Libby asked Caleb.

"Follow me," he whispered and led Libby and Peter back through the front door.

Once outside, Caleb slipped behind a stagecoach that had just come in. Being careful to keep something between them and the inn, Libby and Peter followed Caleb to the side of the building. When they worked their way around to the back, they saw Jordan near the stable.

As he glanced their way, Peter signed *Danger ahead!* Jordan disappeared into the stable. With their faces turned away from the windows of the inn, Libby, Caleb, and Peter crossed the backyard.

When Caleb was sure they were out of the swindler's sight, he picked up his pace. All the way to the railroad station, they walked fast but tried to look as if they weren't hurrying.

The minute Jordan caught up with them, they turned toward

the home of Dr. Brown. On the way there, Caleb suddenly stopped in the middle of the road. "Jordan, is that your stomach I hear rumbling?"

Jordan stopped next to him. "My stomach is growling like a hound dog. I feel like I ain't had nourishment in days."

Just thinking about food, Libby felt starved. "Maybe Dr. Brown will give us some lunch."

About three blocks from the depot, Libby saw a brick house with a shed attached to the back side.

"That must be it!" Libby exclaimed. "If Dr. Brown is a leader in the Underground Railroad, he'll know what we should do next."

Across the road in front of the house was a thick woods. Caleb started toward the trees, and the rest of them followed. They were partway there when Libby heard the sound of horses trotting along the road.

Instantly Libby and the boys raced for the woods. They had barely slipped inside the line of trees when a buggy of the kind used by doctors came into view. When Libby noticed a medical bag at the driver's feet, she felt sure it was Dr. Brown. Beside him sat a woman wearing a long black dress, white gloves, and a hat.

Dr. Brown stopped on the road in front of the house. Quickly he climbed down and walked around to the woman on the other side of the buggy. When he offered his hand, she stood up.

She's tall for a woman, Libby thought, watching her. *And awkward, too, about handling her skirts.*

A veil covered her face, no doubt making it hard for her to see. She had difficulty on the step down.

Reaching the ground, the woman started toward the house with the doctor walking beside her. Leaving Libby and Peter in the woods, Caleb and Jordan hurried toward the house. They had crossed the road into the front lawn when Libby heard the pounding of hooves. As though the woman also heard the galloping horse, she turned around.

In the direction from which the doctor had come, a cloud of dust rose along the road. Within moments a rider galloped into sight. Two more riders followed not far behind.

For one second Jordan froze. As though forgetting where she was, the woman stared at him. Then Caleb grabbed Jordan's arm, and the boys broke into a run, heading back to the woods.

Again Dr. Brown and the woman hurried toward the front door. Before they reached it, the lead rider reined in his horse. When Libby saw his face, she knew the worst had happened. *The slavetrader, Riggs!*

Then the man kicked his horse and rode straight toward Jordan. "I said you'd never get away!" Riggs shouted at him. "Now I've got you, boy!"

His eyes filled with terror, Jordan looked up. In that instant a man's voice cried out, "Run, Jordan! Run!"

14

The Heat of the Furnace

Startled, Riggs turned his horse toward the house. A confused look crossed his face. Only a doctor and a woman stood before him—a woman in a long black dress and a hat. Yet from behind the veil a man's voice had spoken.

Then Jordan leaped into action, again racing toward the woods. As Riggs started after him, the woman cried out, a great, deep bellow.

Once more Riggs wheeled his horse to stare at the woman. In that moment she began to run in the opposite direction from Jordan. As she started around the house, she stumbled. When she caught up her long skirts, a man's pant legs showed underneath.

Again kicking his horse, Riggs started after the man disguised as a woman. Suddenly Jordan stopped, as though unsure what to do.

"Go, Jordan!" the man commanded again, and Jordan went. A moment later he disappeared into the woods.

Just then the two other riders galloped up. As the man in a dress fled across the yard, the slave catchers followed. When they reached him, the catchers leaped from their horses.

One of the catchers tripped the fleeing man. The other shoved his face into the ground. As the hat and veil fell away, Libby saw a man's short black hair.

Is that Jordan's father, Micah Parker? Libby wondered. Who else would have known Jordan's name?

While one slave catcher twisted the man's arms behind him, the other snapped leg-irons around his ankles. As Jordan's daddy lay on the ground, Riggs rode over next to him.

Gazing down at the runaway, Riggs gloated, "I came for your boy and got you—an even bigger prize!"

Even from where she hid, Libby could hear Dr. Brown's groan. As if suddenly remembering him, Riggs turned his horse that way.

"So! This will teach you not to help a runaway slave!"

But Dr. Brown seemed not to hear. As the slave catchers yanked Jordan's father to his feet, the doctor shuddered. "Stop it!"

But Riggs only laughed. "I'll whip him till he obeys. Then I'll get big money for him!"

Dragging Jordan's father by the arms, the slave catchers threw him facedown over a horse.

"Let him go!" Dr. Brown commanded. "You'll kill the man!"

But Riggs towered over the doctor. "Just wait!" he threatened. "I'll find the magistrate and be back to arrest you!"

Wheeling his horse, Riggs rode away. The two slave catchers followed with one of them leading the horse that carried Micah Parker.

As Dr. Brown watched them go, he started to tremble. The moment Riggs and the catchers were out of sight, a girl about Libby's age hurried out of the house. The girl's hair was braided in two long pigtails.

"Let's talk to Dr. Brown before he goes inside," Caleb said.

Libby and Peter followed him out of the woods. As they started across the road, the girl spoke.

"C'mon, Papa," she said. "They're gone for now."

Taking her father by the arm, she led him toward the front door. Just before they reached the steps, the doctor looked around and saw Libby, Caleb, and Peter.

"Who are you?" the doctor asked.

"Jordan's friends," Caleb told him.

The doctor motioned to them. "Come in." He waited at the door for them to enter, then said, "This is my daughter Frances."

Once inside, the doctor seemed to have new life. "Send for help," he told Frances.

"The men who would rescue a fugitive aren't here. They left town just before you came."

As though unwilling to believe her words, the doctor sank into a chair. "They're really gone?"

His daughter nodded. "I don't know what happened, but I saw them ride off together."

Covering his face with his hands, the doctor began to weep. Her arms around his shoulders, Frances stood next to him.

When at last Dr. Brown looked up, his face was lined with tears. "I never lost a passenger before. What will happen to the poor man?"

"Please, sir." Caleb spoke softly. "I'm afraid for Micah too. But I've got to find Jordan. When the slave catchers went after his father, Jordan got away from me."

Dr. Brown drew a long, shaky breath. As if he had trained himself to think no matter what was going on, he said, "You can't go now."

"But I must," Caleb answered. "Jordan will go crazy thinking about what happened to his father. He'll do something stupid, something—"

Dr. Brown held up his hand, silencing Caleb. "Our woods are thick with many places to hide. There's an Indian trail Jordan can follow if necessary. About a mile from here, there's a creek. He'll find water."

"But I've got to find Jordan before the slave catchers do." Caleb's face showed the pain and worry he felt.

"One person can hide much easier than two or three or four.

Any minute now, the slave catchers will be back with the magistrate. If you leave, you'll lead the catchers to Jordan."

As if accepting the truth in the doctor's words, Caleb dropped down, sitting cross-legged on the floor. But every muscle of his body showed his desire to be off.

"The minute it's safe, I'll go into the woods," Frances promised Caleb as she fed everyone. "I know all the hiding places. I'll find your friend."

"What's going on?" Peter asked Libby.

With all that had happened, she had forgotten to tell him. Taking the slate from his bag, she started to write.

"What's a magistrate?" Peter asked finally.

Caleb was the one who explained. "A justice, a judge," he wrote on the slate. "He decides who's doing right and who's doing wrong."

When they finished eating, Frances led them across a hallway into a small sitting room. "When the slave catchers come back, hide in here so they don't recognize you later."

Frances showed Libby a small boxlike table with slatted doors. "If you crawl in there, you can see what's going on, but they can't see you."

In a surprisingly short period of time Riggs returned. When he pounded on the door, Libby and Caleb jumped up. His eyes wide with fear, Peter followed them into the sitting room.

While Caleb and Peter slipped behind heavy drapes, Libby crawled into the small table. As soon as Libby knelt in place, Frances closed the doors. By peering through the narrow cracks between the slats, Libby could see through the hallway into the parlor.

When Dr. Brown opened the front door, Riggs swaggered in. A kind-looking gentleman followed him.

"Mr. Gilson will see that justice is done," the slavetrader announced.

As the person who decided the outcome of cases brought into court, the magistrate was expected to carry out the law. However, Mr. Gilson looked very unhappy about being there.

"Well, what are you waiting for?" Riggs demanded when the magistrate did nothing. "I've given you the proof you need!"

His gaze steady and unafraid, Mr. Gilson watched the slave-trader but did not answer.

The magistrate's unwillingness to obey angered Riggs. "I caught this so-called doctor helping a slave escape. You saw that slave for yourself. He's still in the front yard. Arrest this man!"

"I cannot arrest him." Judge Gilson spoke in a calm, steady voice.

"You can't arrest him?" Riggs raged. "That's your job!"

"But this is Sunday," the judge answered.

"Sunday? What does that have to do with it?"

"This is the Lord's day. I make no arrests on Sunday." Without a backward glance, Mr. Gilson walked out of the house.

Riggs followed him, shouting all the way to the road. Dr. Brown quietly closed the door, then locked it.

On her hands and knees, Libby crawled out from the table and crept over to a window. Being careful to stay behind a curtain, she and Caleb and Peter watched. Frances and her father watched from another window.

Micah Parker was still slung over the horse. A chain stretched between the iron bands around his ankles.

"It must be agony for Jordan's father to lie on his stomach that way," Libby said.

Caleb agreed. "Every time the horse moves, he feels it."

Moments later one of the slave catchers pulled Micah Parker down from the horse. With quick, angry movements, the catcher bound a rope around Micah's hands. Holding the long end of the rope, the catcher climbed up on the horse.

When the two slave catchers rode away, Jordan's father walked behind. Swinging his feet as wide as the chain would allow, he brought forward one foot, then another, trying to keep up.

Libby cringed just watching him. "If he stumbles and falls, they'll drag him!"

On his horse again, Riggs waited in the middle of the road

until Micah Parker and the slave catchers disappeared from sight. Then, with one last angry look at Dr. Brown's house, Riggs rode off in the opposite direction.

"What's he going to do?" Libby asked Caleb.

"Get together a bunch of slave catchers and go after Jordan."

Libby's mind was still reeling from all that had happened. For months Jordan had longed to see his father.

Caleb turned from the window. "I'm going now," he told Dr. Brown. "I've got to find Jordan before dark."

As though he had aged ten years, the doctor again sank into his chair. "Do everything you can to bring Jordan back. If you manage to get him this far, we'll keep him safe."

To Libby the doctor's quiet voice seemed even more heartbreaking than all the angry shouting she had heard.

Libby, Caleb, and Peter followed Frances into the kitchen. Working together, they made more sandwiches. Quickly they wrapped them in pieces of cloth. Then Frances told them the best way to search the woods. She and Peter would take one half. Libby and Caleb would search the other half. They would try to move without sound, yet show themselves plainly so that Jordan wouldn't be frightened.

As quietly as possible, Libby and Caleb walked through their half of the woods. Whenever they came to a cluster of bushes or a clump of trees, they searched carefully. At even a small hollow in the ground, Caleb checked to see if Jordan lay hidden beneath a pile of old, fallen leaves. By the time Libby and Caleb came out on the far side of the woods, the sun lay close to the western horizon.

"We have to find him soon!" Caleb muttered as they started back through the woods.

As they continued searching, the dusk grew deeper. Even Caleb showed his panic now by whispering, "Once it's dark, we'll *never* see him!"

Walking back from a different direction, they noticed a large log they had missed before. Dropping down on her hands and knees, Libby wiggled under bushes to reach the far side of the log. There, in a hollow beneath the wood, Jordan was huddled.

The moment Libby motioned to him, Caleb crawled under the bushes. With his forehead on the ground, Jordan turned his head just enough to see Caleb. Reaching out, Caleb rested his hand on his friend's shoulder.

"I'm sorry," he said quietly.

As if he didn't recognize Caleb, Jordan only stared at him.

"Come with us," Caleb said.

His face swollen from weeping and his eyes glazed with grief, Jordan shook his head.

"You need to hide," Caleb told him.

But Jordan pulled away, as if wanting nothing to do with Caleb.

Again Caleb spoke quietly. "We need to hurry," he warned. "The slave catchers will find you."

Jordan's eyes were wild now. "Maybe they'd take me to where my daddy be. Maybe I'd see him again!"

"That's exactly what your daddy doesn't want!" Caleb exclaimed.

Jordan shuddered. "How could my daddy give himself away for me? How could he give up his life for mine?"

Still on his knees, Jordan pounded the earth with his fists. "Momma needs him. Serena and Zack and little Rose—they all need him. If my daddy hadn't called out to me, he would have gotten away!"

Caleb tugged at Jordan's arm. "You need to hide."

Instead, Jordan's shoulders heaved with sobs. "Just when I found my daddy, I lost him again!"

"Your daddy wants you to be *free*!"

Only then did Jordan seem to understand. Slowly he crawled out from his hiding place, got to his feet, and followed Caleb.

As they started back, the darkness grew thick around them. To Libby's relief Caleb remembered the direction they should go. Partway through the woods, they met Peter and Frances. From then on Frances took the lead.

When they drew close to the house, Frances brought them

around to where they could see the backyard. A lighted lantern stood on a post, giving the all-clear signal. Crossing the open yard, Frances took them into the house.

Inside, she led them up the stairs to the second floor. At the top of the steps was a short hallway. At the end of the hall, Frances opened a secret door into the attic.

"Hurry!" she whispered to Jordan. "If someone comes, there's another door. It leads into the upper floor of our shed. You'll be safe there."

Later that evening Libby heard Dr. Brown talking to Caleb. "If you and Jordan suddenly need my horses, take them," the doctor said. "Horse flesh has little value compared to a human life."

"Thank you, sir," Caleb answered. "I'll have a look at them now."

As Caleb slipped out of the house, Libby saw Jordan sitting on the stairs, listening.

"I don't understand what happened," she told Dr. Brown. "Why didn't the magistrate arrest you?"

"Mr. Gilson knows me well," the doctor answered. "He believes in what I'm doing."

"And he's supposed to uphold a fugitive slave law that goes against everything he believes?"

Dr. Brown nodded. "He's in a hard place. When a law made by man goes against the ways of God, it brings all kinds of trouble."

Having Pa caught with a fugitive was the nightmare Libby dreaded. "If you're thrown in jail, what will your family do?" she asked Dr. Brown. "When you know what might happen, how can you keep on helping fugitives?"

"How can I *not* help them?" he answered. "God's law is higher than that of men."

God's law is higher? Libby thought. *That's what Mrs. Hunter said. What does it mean?*

Standing up, the doctor crossed to where a large Bible lay on a table. "Come here, Libby."

The pages were open to the twenty-third chapter of the book of Deuteronomy. Dr. Brown pointed to the words. "Thou shalt not deliver unto his master the servant which is escaped from his master unto thee."

Libby put the verse in her own words. "If a slave has taken refuge with you, don't turn him over to his master."

Dr. Brown's gaze met hers. "Should I obey someone who sees a fellow human being as a piece of property? Or should I obey God? He loves every slave exactly the way He loves me."

As though wanting to make sure Libby didn't misunderstand, Dr. Brown explained it again. "When two laws are in conflict with each other, God's law is more important—more to be followed."

Turning, the doctor saw Jordan listening from the stairs. When the doctor walked over and rested his hand on the boy's shoulder, Jordan flinched.

Dr. Brown stepped back. "You must find it hard to trust anyone right now. I cannot tell you how sorry I am about your father. When it's safe, we'll take you to the next place."

"I can't go on." Jordan's voice broke. "I can't leave my daddy behind."

"We'll do what we can to help him," the doctor promised. "But when it's time, you must go, like your daddy said. You can't let his sacrifice be wasted."

Soon after Jordan returned to the attic, Frances picked up the large Bible. As she started up the stairs, Libby followed her.

"Mama and the rest of our family are gone right now," Frances explained. "Whenever I get a chance, I read Bible stories to fugitives. They love to hear them."

When Frances opened the carefully hidden door, Libby followed her into the attic room.

To Libby's surprise she found other fugitives there besides Jordan. When they had arrived, Libby didn't know. But a mother and father and their two young children sat on blankets on the floor.

Pulling a lamp close, Frances opened the Bible to the story of Daniel's three friends. Because they believed in the living God, they refused to bow down and worship an image made of gold.

As Frances read the story of how the three young men stood against the king's orders, Jordan and the other fugitives sat without moving or making a sound. When the young men were thrown into the fiery furnace, the eyes of the children grew large. When God delivered the men from the flames, the children clapped their hands and giggled.

They know what it means, Libby thought. *Even the small ones have felt the heat of the furnace.*

Like the others, Jordan seemed to find comfort. But when Frances finished reading, a thoughtful look remained in Jordan's eyes.

That night Libby slept in the same room as Frances, while Caleb, Jordan, and Peter stayed in the upper floor of the shed. The moment Libby lay down, she remembered all that had happened to Micah Parker. The more she thought about him, the more upset she felt.

Again she seemed to hear the father's warning cry to his son. Again she saw Jordan's terror, his grieving for his daddy. Knowing she must, Libby tried to sort things out.

I'm scared that Pa might lose his boat, she thought. *But Elijah Lovejoy lost his life. Jordan's father gave up his freedom for his son.*

Libby's thoughts became a prayer. *I want something worth living for, Lord. Something real—something worthwhile.*

But that seems so big, God—so hard—even impossible. Can you help me choose what counts most?

Then the long days without much sleep caught up to Libby, and she drifted off.

She woke to the sound of a light tapping on the bedroom

door. Three even knocks, a space, then three raps again. *Caleb's signal! But it's still night.*

Then as she came awake, she knew. *Something is wrong!*

She had no way of knowing how long she had slept. Through the window she saw the moon riding high in the sky. Softly she rapped back. Long, short, long. Then she fumbled in the dark to find her clothes.

Quickly Libby changed into her dress, snatched up her shoes, and tiptoed to the door. Out in the hall, she closed the door again without making a sound.

Caleb waited there, a shape darker than the night. Walking at one side of the steps to avoid any creak, he and Libby clung to the railing to find their way down. At the bottom of the steps, Caleb led her into the parlor.

"Jordan is gone!" Caleb whispered when it was safe.

"Gone?"

"Disappeared!" Caleb sounded as upset as Libby had ever heard him. "He's nowhere to be found!"

15

The Disappearing Package

"But why?" Libby forgot to whisper. "How could Jordan disappear?"

"I don't know. He slipped away while I was sleeping. There's a door in the shed that leads outside. It would have been easy for him to leave."

In that moment there was something Libby remembered. "It's what you said. The place where Jordan doesn't have good judgment. When he's scared about his family."

Caleb agreed. "I think he's hunting for his father. If he is, he's risking his own freedom. And maybe his life."

"What can we do?" Libby asked.

"Try to follow Jordan." In the darkness Caleb fumbled for a match. When he lit a lamp, he kept the flame low. Taking a quill pen, he scratched a note.

Valuable package disappeared. We are looking for it. Caleb and Libby

As Caleb turned down the flame, it flickered, then died. In the darkness he and Libby waited, listening. In that moment a clock started chiming.

Libby counted the strokes. "Eleven o'clock," she whispered at last. "Jordan can't have been gone more than an hour."

In the silence Libby and Caleb crept through the kitchen. The side door swung open on well-oiled hinges. Again they stopped to listen and peer into the darkness.

After a moment they slipped outside. Keeping to the deepest shadows, Caleb led Libby to the barn. The top half of the door was open. Caleb opened the bottom half, and they crept in, again without sound.

Standing just inside the door, Libby waited for her eyes to adjust to the even deeper darkness. When she saw the first stall was empty, she remembered Dr. Brown's words. *If you and Jordan need my horses, use them.*

At the time Libby had wondered how he could be so free with such valuable property. Now she understood. Jordan must have taken the doctor at his word.

Through the open door, the moon gave little light. Yet within a moment Caleb moved forward. As if he had been there earlier and memorized where things were, he felt along the wall.

When he passed where Libby stood, she saw only the dark outline of a bridle in his hand. Yet without hesitating, Caleb walked into the second stall. Talking quietly to the horse, he slipped on the bridle. When the saddle was in place, Caleb led the horse out of the stall.

"That's the way, Annie." Where there was more light, Caleb checked to be sure he had everything right. "We're just going for a ride." Grabbing a lead rope, Caleb wrapped it around his waist.

Outside the barn, he stayed on the grass to deaden the sound of hooves. Leading Annie, he walked quickly to the woods with Libby following. Under the covering of trees, the night was even darker. Again Libby had the feeling that Caleb had memorized the way. Before long her feet felt the smoothness of packed dirt.

The Indian path, Libby thought, remembering the trail she had seen when searching for Jordan.

Caleb swung up into the saddle, then reached down to help Libby up. The moment she was seated behind him, Caleb lifted the reins. Annie moved out in a steady trot. With her arms around Caleb's waist, Libby hung on.

"How do you know where Jordan went?" she asked Caleb when she thought it was safe to speak.

"I don't know," Caleb said. "But I heard Jordan ask Frances where she thought the slave catchers took his father. She told him the Indian trail might be the shortest way to the Mississippi. I think it's thirteen or fourteen miles."

"Jordan's father was walking," Libby said. "The slave catchers couldn't gallop with him behind."

"And Jordan was riding. He could find them," Caleb said. "Especially if his father tried to slow down the slave catchers."

For some time Caleb and Libby rode in the darkness. The farther they went, the more afraid Libby felt.

"I'm scared, Caleb," she said finally. "If the slave catchers see Jordan—"

Caleb turned his head to answer. "I know." He spoke softly, and Libby had no doubt that he was worried too.

"What if we make things worse?" she asked. "What if we come up behind Jordan when he can't see us? We could scare him into jumping out of hiding."

Caleb shrugged, as if he had thought of the same thing. "But he might need our help. We have to try," he said, as if that settled the matter.

Before long, Libby began to feel every movement of the horse. *I never learned to ride,* she thought. Trying to ignore how uncomfortable she felt, she kept looking around.

For some distance they rode with a canopy of tall trees arching above them. Whenever they drew close to a home or farm, Caleb slowed Annie to a walk. When needed, he rode around a house and found the path on the other side.

A couple of hours had passed when Libby first caught the

scent of the river. Like the sweetness of air after a rain, the river breeze felt cool and refreshing. Soon Caleb slowed the horse again. Moving even more quietly, he stopped Annie often to listen.

The trail was wider here, as if many people used it to come to a river crossing. Staying away from the bushes that reached out from either side, Caleb kept to the center of the track. He leaned forward to whisper in Annie's ear, urging the horse on. At last they came to the banks of the Mississippi.

Within the line of trees that grew close to the water, Caleb slid off the horse. When he helped Libby down, she stumbled and nearly fell. Quickly Caleb grabbed her arm to steady her, but he did not speak.

So sore that she could barely move, Libby wondered how she could possibly run if it became necessary. Waiting and watching, Caleb kept Annie a short distance from the edge of the trees.

Without moving a muscle, Libby stood there, afraid that any small sound would give them away to the wrong person. Here, where the trees gave way to the wide river, she could see the moon again. To her relief it was still high in the sky.

Then from across the water, Libby heard a sound and strained to see. Islands dotted the river, darker shapes that merged with the darkness of the water. Grabbing Caleb's arm, Libby pointed. When he nodded, she knew that he, too, had heard the noise.

In that moment Libby remembered how easily sounds carried over water. The person making the noise could be quite far away.

When she heard the sound again, Libby knew what it was—oars creaking in their locks. Whoever was rowing made no effort at silence. That could mean only one thing. It would not be fugitives or people helping fugitives. Whoever was in that boat had to be slave catchers.

"Keep watching," Caleb whispered into Libby's ear. "I'm taking Annie farther back." Disappearing between the trees, Caleb was soon lost to view.

As time dragged out, Libby waited, still straining to see. Then at the end of an island, something moved. In the light of the moon, the shape grew longer, as if moving out of the shadow of the island. Between that island and the next, Libby saw the shape turn into a rowboat heading upstream.

Is Jordan's daddy in that boat? Libby wondered.

For only a moment he had stood tall. As Libby remembered the leg-irons around his ankles and the chains between his feet, she thought of Hattie, Serena, Zack, and little Rose.

I can't cry, Libby told herself. *I've got to listen, think, pray.*

Pray. On the night wind, the word broke into her grieving heart. *Why am I standing here doing nothing when I could be praying?*

She began by praying for Jordan. *Wherever he is, Lord, take care of him. Tell him what to do.* She went on to pray for Jordan's father. *O Lord, give him a way to escape!*

In that moment Libby felt peaceful, as though others were praying with her. Was Dr. Brown lying awake, praying even now? And Frances, Jordan, Caleb, Micah Parker himself? Perhaps even his wife, Hattie, had sensed she needed to pray.

Barely had the thought crossed her mind than Libby heard another sound in the darkness. The soft whinny of a horse.

Libby stiffened. What if there were other slave catchers around? If they heard Annie, they would have no problem following the sound to Caleb.

There it was again. A second whinny. Libby's stomach muscles tightened. *What's wrong? Caleb should be farther back.*

Turning from the waterfront, Libby tried to follow Caleb into the darkness. But when she heard a soft movement—a movement where Caleb shouldn't be—Libby knew.

It wasn't Annie. Someone else is here with me in these dark woods!

When she sensed the movement again, Libby's fists clenched in terror. Frantically she looked around for a hiding place, trying to blend with the night.

Then a whisper reached her. "Libby!"

At first she thought she had imagined it.

"Libby!" came the whisper again, even closer this time.

In relief Libby sagged against the tree. It was Jordan. Jordan whispering in the night. They had found him after all! Or rather, he had found them.

Not far behind was Caleb. He and Jordan had taken the horses farther back to a small opening in the trees, leaving them where there was grass.

Now Jordan led Libby and Caleb to the riverbank. As he, Libby, and Caleb knelt down behind the trees closest to the water, the night exploded with sound. First a splash, then oars knocked against a boat.

"Get him!" a rough voice exclaimed.

"I can't!"

"Yes, you can. Go after him."

"I can't swim. You go."

"I can't swim either. We'll both have to get him. The minute he comes up, hold out an oar. He'll be glad for our help."

"No, he won't!" Jordan whispered.

"Where'd he go?" asked the voice across the water. "Where is he?" The man was worried now. "There ain't nobody who can swim with leg-irons on."

"I tell you, he's gotta come up at least once."

"No, he doesn't!" Excitement filled Jordan's whisper. "My daddy can swim longer underwater than anyone I know."

"Riggs ain't gonna like this" came a voice. "This here property was valuable. We ain't got no way to prove that he drowned."

"If we can't find him, we ain't gonna get paid!"

The men were silent then, waiting. Again the oars knocked against the boat. Then Libby heard the sound of an oar dropping into its lock. Straining forward, she watched. As the moonlight fell upon the boat, Libby saw it was moving again, making circles as if going around and around a certain spot.

Off to the right something else lay in the darkness. Another boat? Libby tried to decide what it could be. *Almost as long as a rowboat, but not the right shape.*

Suddenly Jordan caught his breath and pointed to where Libby had been looking. Whatever they were seeing, it was rounded on the top and solid looking. Now it seemed to be moving—slowly, slowly moving.

"A log!" Caleb's whisper was no more than a breath, but he, too, was filled with wonder. "A large floating log!"

As the men in the boat rowed around in circles, the log slowly moved away from them. Always moving slightly downstream, it seemed to drift with the current.

By now Jordan was so excited he could hardly contain himself. Then Libby noticed what he had already seen. The log was stripped of bark, rubbed clean and smooth by the washing of water. On the side of the log away from the slave catchers, Libby saw a man's head.

Then an arm and hand reached forward in a swimming stroke. With each stroke the log moved closer to shore. Riding the current, it was going downstream from where Libby and the boys watched.

Quietly Jordan stood up. Hiding behind trees and bushes, he crept downriver, with Libby and Caleb following. Staying even with the log, Jordan watched as it drew closer and closer to shore. When at last the log bumped against the riverbank, Jordan was as near as he could be without coming out into the open.

For a minute Micah Parker waited, clinging to a broken-off branch on the side of the log. From where she knelt, Libby saw him draw long, deep breaths. With his face turned toward the riverbank, he seemed to be deciding how to cross the open ground.

Then Micah let go of the branch. On hands and knees he crawled up the riverbank.

Just then the men on the river stopped their circling and turned the boat toward shore.

"Daddy!" Jordan whispered.

His father's head jerked up. In the light of the moon, Libby saw the light in Micah's eyes.

But Jordan was frantic now. "The're coming this way!"

16

Big Bullies

Micah Parker turned toward the river. After one glance he kept his head low. On his belly now, he pushed with his toes and pulled himself forward with his elbows.

When the chain between his ankles clanked, Micah stopped. He turned his head, as if to listen. As he moved on, he again pulled himself with his elbows but dragged his feet in the dirt. At last Micah reached the edge of the woods.

Without wasting a moment, Jordan started crawling back into the woods. On his hands and knees again, his daddy kept up. Twigs and branches reached out, catching the chain between his ankles. But Jordan and Micah kept on, with Libby and Caleb following.

Deeper within the woods, Jordan stood up, but his father kept crawling. Soon there came the sound of a boat grating against the gravel at the edge of the water. The men's angry voices came clearly through the trees.

Jordan stopped, standing without movement, and the rest stopped behind him.

"Riggs ain't gonna like this!" The voice came from the direction of the trail through the woods.

"It's all your fault. You should have watched him better."

"Watched him? How should I know he'd jump into the river?"

Then the men passed by, and their voices moved farther away. At last Jordan walked on, with his father still crawling on his hands and knees behind him.

"If we could just get rid of your leg-irons," Jordan muttered. Libby knew it would take a blacksmith or a sledgehammer and chisel to break the chain that stretched between the bands around each ankle.

As they reached more open ground, Micah stood up. Swinging his legs as far apart as the chain allowed, he brought forward one foot, then another. When they came to the small clearing, Micah Parker waited while Jordan brought the mare he had ridden over to a stump.

"How did you find me?" Micah whispered to him. "How did you ever find me?"

"I prayed," Jordan said quietly. "The Lord showed me where to go."

With the moonlight streaming down on his son, Jordan's daddy just looked at him. "You has grown since I seen you. You be a man now."

Jordan shook his head. "I ain't a man yet, Daddy."

But his father looked deep into his eyes. "You all right, Jordan?"

Jordan straightened in the proud look that made him seem like royalty. "Now that you're here, I am as right as I can be."

Jordan and Caleb helped Micah onto the horse. Then Jordan swung up in front of his father. With his legs swinging down on one side, Micah hung on to his son's shoulder. Lifting the reins, Jordan turned the horse toward an opening in the trees.

"Your momma?" Micah asked softly. "Serena, Zack, and little Rose?"

"They're wanting with all their hearts to see you, Daddy."

With Libby and Caleb on Annie again, they rode onto the

trail. Here the path was wide enough for Libby and Caleb to ride alongside.

His voice still soft, Micah spoke to his son. "You didn't run, did you?"

Jordan turned, his gaze clinging to his father's face. "At first I did, Daddy. I could only think what you told me to do."

Jordan's father nodded with approval. "That's my son."

"But I couldn't leave you." Jordan's voice broke. "I had to find you."

When the trail grew narrow, Caleb signaled Annie to fall behind Jordan and his father. While still some distance from the Brown house, he and Jordan stopped their horses. "We can't take a chance on having a whinny give away Jordan and his father," Caleb whispered to Libby.

At a well-hidden spot, all of them worked together taking handfuls of grass and leaves to rub down the horses. Then Caleb tied Annie's lead rope to a tree. Leaving the other horse nearby, the four of them set off through the woods. Again Jordan's daddy stretched his chain to the limit, swinging one foot ahead of the other.

In the darkness before dawn, they reached Brighton. To Libby's great relief, the lantern in Dr. Brown's backyard was lit. The minute Caleb drew near the house, Dr. Brown opened the door. When he saw Micah Parker, his face lit up.

"I can't tell you how glad I am to see you!" Drawing all of them inside, the doctor closed and locked the door.

When he turned up the flame of a lamp, he noticed Micah's wet clothes. "You jumped overboard and swam with leg-irons on?" The doctor was amazed. "Just the weight of those irons would drag the average swimmer down—let alone the strong river currents."

But there would be no changing of clothes until the irons were off. "I'll get you to my friend the blacksmith," Dr. Brown said. "Do the slave catchers know you're alive?"

"If they find my marks in the riverbank, they be knowin'," Micah answered.

Caleb groaned. "We should have brushed them out." Yet there had been no time.

"You need to leave right now while it's still dark," Dr. Brown told Micah. "Riggs promised me another call. He'll come with a search warrant and more slave catchers."

Standing at one side, the doctor looked through a narrow crack between the window and a heavy curtain. "I see the light at the Hill House," he said, talking about the stagecoach inn where Libby and the boys had come in.

By road Dr. Brown's house was about five blocks away from the Hill House. In a straight line, the inn was closer, with only a few buildings between. None of those buildings blocked the view of the signal light.

"It's safe for you to go on," Dr. Brown told Jordan's father. "Sit down for a minute while I tell you what to do."

As all of them gathered around the kitchen table, Dr. Brown explained to Micah, "We have three stagecoach stops in the area. They all work together and with the Underground Railroad people in private homes. An hour ago I hitched up our old mule in case you got back. I'll drive you to the stable at the Hill House. There's a blacksmith there who will take off your leg-irons.

"The minute you're free of them, try to go four blocks north to the Palmer House." On the table Dr. Brown drew a line with his finger. "If you need to stop there, go in the cellar door. They have tunnels under the yard where fugitives hide. But if you're able to keep on, walk another mile or so. You'll come to a T in the road. Turn left and walk to the Andrews house. It's a large private home with a cupola on the roof. If there's a lighted lantern in the cupola, it's safe to go up to the door."

"And if there be slave catchers around those places?" Micah asked.

"The last Underground Railroad station in the area is another stagecoach stop, the Hart House. It's about half a mile beyond the Andrews family. If you need to hide and don't see someone to help you, crawl into their cistern. It's dry."

As though about to set off on a great adventure, Micah

grinned. But then the doctor spoke to Jordan. "You need to take a different route."

"Sir," Jordan said respectfully. "My daddy and I want to stay together."

"If you do, you'll be caught for sure," Dr. Brown warned. "Both of you are marked fugitives. Every slave catcher for miles around will know you want to be together."

Pleading in his eyes, Jordan turned to his father. "Daddy—"

But Micah agreed with Dr. Brown. "If we go different ways, at least one of us should get back to your momma."

"You could meet at Springfield," the doctor told them. "There's a group of free blacks there who will help you. If you ask for the Colored Baptist Church, you'll find the people you need."

"That sounds like a good meeting place for all of us," Caleb said quickly. Digging into his pocket, he gave Jordan's father one of the railroad passes from Mr. Godfrey. "With this you can get on or off a train whenever you need to."

Standing up, Micah clapped his son's shoulder in a good-bye. Jordan trembled but did not speak. When Micah left the room, Jordan watched his daddy as if seeing him for the last time.

The minute Dr. Brown and Micah went out the door, Caleb turned to Frances. "What's the quickest way to get Jordan out of town?"

"The railroad. The real railroad, I mean. The St. Louis, Alton and Chicago train to Springfield. But it costs a lot of money for a ticket."

"I've got more passes." Again Caleb dug into his pocket, this time giving a ticket to Jordan. "Compliments of Mr. Godfrey," he said.

When Frances saw the pass, her eyes lit up. Standing at one side of the window, she looked through the narrow crack to the Hill House.

"Go now while it's still dark," she told Jordan. "At the inn they'll hide you, give you breakfast, and put you on the next train."

After a quick thank-you to Frances, Jordan slipped out the door. As Caleb and Libby again sat down at the table, she looked around the kitchen. To her the room offered warmth and security, something she needed right now.

With the ease of long practice, Frances broke eggs into a bowl, then poured them into a frying pan. Lifting a lid on the wood cookstove, she set the pan into the opening to speed up the cooking. Watching her, Libby felt glad for this twelve-year-old girl. In spite of all the frightening things in her life, she did what was needed, and even read Bible stories to fugitives.

But Libby felt a nervousness Frances didn't show. "What do we do?" Libby asked Caleb. "If we take the same train as Jordan, we can't follow the swindler."

"I'll check on Dexter this morning," Caleb promised. "With all that's happened, he might already be gone."

Libby swallowed hard. "If we lose Dexter now, we might lose him forever. Today is August third. In twelve days Pa has to have the money. If he doesn't get it, he loses the *Christina*."

"I know," Caleb answered. "I've been counting the days too. And Jordan needs to find the money stolen from his church. But we might have to make a choice."

"Between finding the money and helping Jordan?"

Caleb nodded. "I'm afraid so."

"By the way," Libby said. "Where's Peter?"

Caleb jumped up. "Still sleeping, I bet." From the sound of it, Caleb took the stairs two at a time.

In that moment Libby remembered all the things she needed to explain to Peter. Having a new brother wasn't going to be as easy as she thought.

By the time Caleb returned with the ten-year-old, the eggs were ready, as well as great, thick slices of bread. As if she hadn't eaten in years, Libby devoured everything on her plate. The moment she and the others finished eating, Caleb left for the Hill House. Libby started explaining to Peter.

After filling the slate several times, her fingers felt sore and stiff. Glad for the art lessons she had while living in Chicago,

Libby started drawing quick pictures. When Peter understood, he nodded, and Libby went on. More than once he showed her a sign that would help. As before, Libby felt amazed at how quickly he caught on.

"And we will go to the train Jordan takes?" Peter asked at last.

"Someone at the Hill House will take him there," Libby wrote.

"Will we get on that train?"

All of Libby's questions rushed back. *What about Pa and the* Christina? *What if we don't find the money, and Pa loses the boat?* Libby's stomach tied in a knot just thinking about it. *Do I have to choose between Jordan and what happens to my own father?*

Feeling torn in two directions, Libby didn't want to explain to Peter. Palms up, she shrugged her shoulders.

"If we don't watch out for Jordan, what will happen to him?" Peter asked.

Libby sighed. Ashamed now, she turned away from this younger boy who seemed much older than she.

Jordan and Micah can do more things than any two people I've met, she told herself. *They won't have any trouble reaching a safe place. They don't need us. In fact, we might get in their way.*

In that moment Libby felt tired all over. Going into the sitting room, she curled up in a big chair and closed her eyes. Yet she soon realized that her weariness had nothing to do with being up most of the night.

Though she wanted to sleep, pictures of Jordan flashed through her mind. Jordan on the auction block the day he was sold to Riggs. Jordan walking through the night and the rain, leading his mother and brother and sisters to safety. Jordan kneeling in the woods, weeping for a daddy who had given up his own freedom so that Jordan could be free.

When Caleb returned from the Hill House, he sat down to talk with Libby. "Edward Dexter is still here. He's eating breakfast in the dining room."

"We need to make a choice, don't we?" Libby asked.

Caleb's gaze met hers. "What means the most to us? The money or Jordan?"

Now Libby knew what to answer. "Jordan is our friend. What if we leave him now and something more goes wrong?"

With a promise to write to each other, Libby and Frances said good-bye. Then Libby, Caleb, and Peter walked to the Brighton Depot. As they waited to board the train, Peter asked, "What's that big wooden thing on the front of the engine?"

Taking the slate, Caleb explained. "It's a cowcatcher. Cows wander loose on the prairie. They cause trouble for the trains."

Then Peter wanted to know about the huge water tank next to the tracks.

"The train engine needs water, just like the steam engines on the *Christina*," Caleb wrote. "That's why they put such big tanks along the track—and cisterns, too, to store water."

Caleb showed Peter the nearby cistern. About nine feet in diameter, the round concrete tank was set deep in the ground with only the top showing. A flat wooden cover protected the opening and kept people from falling in. A rope attached to a nearby post led under the cover. Libby guessed that the other end of the rope was tied to a bucket for dipping out water.

When they boarded the train, Libby found a place where two seats faced each other. She and Peter sat closest to the window. Caleb sat down next to Libby.

Soon the train whistled for departure. *How will we know if Jordan is on board?* Libby wondered. Then a man rolled a wagon piled high with trunks and boxes over to the baggage car. Leaning forward, Libby watched every move. Soon she saw Jordan slip from behind a trunk into the baggage car.

His face filled with excitement, Peter signed the letter *J*. Libby laughed with relief. They had Jordan with them.

Moments later the engine chugged out of the station. Grateful that all was well, Libby leaned back. Borrowing Peter's slate, she wrote a message for both him and Caleb. "We'll meet Jordan and his father in Springfield and CELEBRATE!"

Peter held up his hands, signing, *Yes! Yes! We're winning!*

A few miles later, he stood up and started forward for a drink of water. When the train lurched, he staggered, then caught hold of the back of a seat. The boys who sat there glared up at Peter.

"Sorry," he said, and moved on. But the two boys, both of them older than Peter, kept watching him.

On a table near the front of the car was a covered bucket with a tin cup hanging nearby. As Peter picked it up, one of the boys started forward. Reaching over Peter's shoulder, he snatched the cup.

Whirling around, Peter grabbed for it. The bully held it high, then tossed it to his friend.

"Uh-oh!" Caleb leaped up from his seat. Libby followed him.

Peter faced the boys with an angry scowl. Automatically he began to sign, his fingers and hands moving rapidly.

The first boy drew back, staring. Then he began to laugh. Poking his friend, the bully wiggled his fingers, imitating Peter.

Suddenly Peter stopped signing. His face flushed with anger, he held up a clenched fist. "You're not going to get the best of me!"

"So! The little boy wants a fight!" the bully cried. "We'll give you one to remember!"

17

Fire!

In the next moment Caleb reached the bully. "No, you won't!" Grabbing hold of his shirt, Caleb twisted the bully around. But the boy's friend threw up his fists, ready to take on both Caleb and Peter.

"What's the matter with you," Caleb demanded, "picking on someone half your age?"

"Get out of here!" the bully cried. "It's none of your business!"

"You're not touching this boy!" Caleb warned.

"Who says?"

"I do! Libby, call the conductor."

Within a minute the conductor was there, and behind him, a man with a bushy beard.

"Tell the engineer to stop," the second man said, speaking with a strong Irish accent. "We'll put the boys off the train."

"You can't do that to us!" the first bully cried.

"You can't pick fights on Mr. Godfrey's train. You have only five or six miles to walk to the nearest town."

As the train clanked to a stop, the Irishman led the boys to an exit. Moments later the two bullies stood at the side of the track, their eyes resentful as they stared after the train.

"Who are you?" Caleb asked when the man returned.

"Allan Pinkerton, at your service. The Pinkerton Detective Agency." He grinned, then repeated his agency's motto. "The Eye That Never Sleeps."

"I've always wanted to meet you," Caleb said.

Quickly Libby wrote on the slate. When Peter understood, he offered his hand, and Mr. Pinkerton shook it.

"Thank you," Peter said solemnly. "I'm glad you were here."

Libby, Caleb, and Peter had just sat down again when Caleb groaned. "I can't believe what I did!"

"What are you talking about?" Libby asked.

"I forgot the horses. How could I be so careless?"

Libby stared at him. "The horses?"

"Dr. Brown's horses. The ones we used to go after Jordan. Remember? We tied their lead ropes to a couple of trees so they wouldn't wander off while Jordan and Micah got into the house. Then things started happening so fast that I forgot to tell Frances where the horses were."

"Oh, Caleb!"

"I left them without food or water."

"Frances will find them," Libby said.

"We hid them in a really good spot. Jordan and I talked about it. We didn't want someone to steal the horses."

"Dr. Brown will find them," Libby said.

But Caleb wasn't sure about that. "I need to get off. I'll catch the next train back to Brighton and meet you in Springfield."

"But that will take hours!"

"Yup! Hours when the Browns might not find their horses. Hours when the horses won't have food and water."

"But what about Riggs?" Libby was upset now. "He's probably still in Brighton, sniffing his way around. He knows you, Caleb. He knows you had something to do with Jordan escaping. Riggs will do anything to stop what you're doing!"

"Libby, the Browns were really kind to all of us. I don't want to hurt them."

"Caleb, it's dangerous for you to go back." Libby's voice was low. "The slave catchers in this area know you now. They know you walked down the streets of Alton with a fugitive slave, acting as if what you were doing was okay."

"I don't have any choice but to go back," Caleb said. "Jordan is safe now. All he has to do is hide in the baggage car until Springfield. Besides, Mr. Pinkerton is here. If there's any trouble, he'll help you."

"If Riggs and the slave catchers can prove you helped two fugitives, they'll get you arrested!"

"And Dr. Brown and his family are risking everything they have to help fugitives."

"Your grandmother, Caleb," Libby reminded, hoping it would stop him from doing what she knew was dangerous.

"Give her my love," Caleb said quietly. "I'll see you at the Colored Baptist Church in Springfield."

At the next stop, Caleb swung down to the platform. As Libby watched through the window, he turned and waved to her and Peter. Then Caleb hurried into the depot.

Soon the great black steam engine chugged out of the station. As the depot behind them grew smaller and smaller, Libby felt lost and alone. She liked being with Caleb. She liked having him for a friend, but it was more than that. Whenever she felt scared, she depended on Caleb for help.

Now Peter gazed out the window, trying to see everything. Libby leaned back. All she could think about was how good her bed on the *Christina* would feel. The railroad car was growing warmer by the minute.

As the train picked up speed, cinders blew in through the open windows. Watching the cinders, Libby remembered stories about them falling onto a railroad bed. Often they lodged in the wooden ties beneath the tracks and flared up when conditions were right. Grass fires were common in areas where trains passed through.

The tinder hot day made Libby feel jumpy. *What if some train dropped a cinder in the wrong place?*

Silly! Libby tried to push the thought away. *You're borrowing trouble.*

Just the same, she didn't like the specks of black dust all over her dress. Peter's shirt already looked dirty. Reaching up, Libby closed the window next to her.

Soon the heat became so unbearable that she opened it again. The hot wind was better than no air at all.

In laying out the railroad to Springfield, Mr. Godfrey had planned a village every ten miles. Between the towns, great areas of level land stretched off in every direction. As Libby settled back, she watched the four- and five-foot-high grass waving in the wind.

Now in the first week of August, the grass was dry, but countless flowers had sprung up across the prairie. More than once Peter pointed, wanting her to see the blue flowers and the white, with now and then a scattering of red.

At the next village, the engine stopped alongside the large tower close to the track. Lowering the spout, a man let water flow from the tank into the tender—the car just behind the engine.

As passengers started to leave the car, Allan Pinkerton stopped to talk to Libby and Peter.

"I'm needing to get off here," he said. "But you'll have no more trouble from bullies."

Inwardly Libby groaned. When Caleb left the train, he had counted on Mr. Pinkerton if she and Peter needed help.

Again Libby tried to push the thought away. *Everything is going fine. In no time at all, we'll be in Springfield. But just in case—*

"There's something else," she said quickly. "We're looking for a swindler who stole money from my pa and from a church in Galena. If we find him, what do we do?"

Mr. Pinkerton rubbed his bushy beard, thinking about it. "If the man stands still long enough for you to accuse him, you'll have to prove you know what you're talking about."

"I can tell you the exact amount of money he took from Pa and Jordan."

"That would help," Mr. Pinkerton said. "But do you know of a way to identify the stolen money?"

"Ink blotches!" Libby exclaimed. "The pastor at Jordan's church said there are ink blotches on about ten of the bills."

Mr. Pinkerton looked pleased. "If you manage to find bills with ink blotches on them, you've got something to go on."

For the first time in their search for the stolen money, Libby felt they were getting somewhere.

Then Mr. Pinkerton offered a warning. "Just don't try something foolish. A foolhardy man rushes in where even angels fear to tread. But a brave man is wise about handling danger. Sure and I'm wishing that the ten toes of your feet steer you clear of trouble."

"We'll be in trouble, all right." In that moment Libby felt sure of it. "Is there some way to get hold of you?"

Reaching into his pocket, Mr. Pinkerton pulled out a card for his Chicago agency. Flipping it over, he wrote an address on the back. "I'll do my best to be in Springfield in a few days. I'll be staying with a friend. You can find me here." Then Mr. Pinkerton was gone.

While workers loaded freight, Libby and Peter watched out the window, studying every passenger who drew close to the train. A man with hunched-over shoulders stood near the baggage car. Wearing the overalls and straw hat of a farm worker, he leaned on a thick wooden stick for support. As the other Negro passengers boarded the train, the man kept looking back down the track. Only when he swung up into the car did Libby see the side of his face.

After the man disappeared, Libby kept thinking about him. Once, she had seen Jordan pretend he was an old man. Without that picture in her mind, she might not have suspected that the worker was Jordan's father. But now a great shout of laughter bubbled up inside of Libby.

Taking Peter's slate, she wrote the good news. "Micah Parker just got into the baggage car."

Peter grinned. "He was the one who looked like an old man?"

Libby wrote quickly on the slate. "I'm sure of it. Jordan and his daddy are SAFE!"

Once again the engine chugged away from the depot. Just thinking about the happy reunion in the baggage car made Libby want to celebrate. What was Jordan thinking right now as he recognized his father?

"Springfield, here we come!" Libby wrote on the slate. "All we have to do is walk off the train and find the Colored Baptist Church."

Libby felt sure that nothing more would go wrong. In Springfield they would all be together again. As soon as Jordan and his father met Hattie and the other children, the family could go where they wanted and begin their new life of freedom.

Then Libby remembered. Even if his family was together, Jordan would never be satisfied until his name was cleared. His name couldn't be cleared until Jordan found the stolen money and turned it over to John Jones.

And Pa. In twelve days Pa needs to make the double payment. If he doesn't, he'll lose the Christina.

Discouraged again, Libby leaned back and closed her eyes. *Isn't there some way we can solve the mystery of the swindler's treasure?*

Like a worm, a thought wiggled its way into Libby's mind. *Jordan and his daddy did just fine without us. We didn't need to get on this train. Caleb and I could have stayed in Brighton and tried to catch the swindler.*

Libby's thoughts went round and round, always coming back to the same place. *We made a stupid choice, and all for nothing!*

Just as Libby drifted off to sleep, Peter poked her. *Quit bothering me,* she thought, half-awake and half-asleep. *Let me be!*

Peter tugged at her arm. "Libby! You've got to look!"

At the sound of panic in his voice, Libby came awake. As she opened her eyes, Peter pointed out the window. Alongside the train, the tall, dry prairie grass swayed back and forth in the wind. But farther ahead and off to the right, flames raced across the top of the grass.

"Fire!" muttered a man just ahead of Libby.

From the front of the car came a woman's cry. "Prairie fire!" Jumping up, people crowded the aisle to look through the windows on the right side.

Brakes squealing, the train came to a stop. Leaning out, Libby saw that the fire wasn't only off away from them. Just ahead of the engine, the grass along the track was scorched black, as if the fire had begun there. Still farther ahead was a trestle with the long bridge that crossed the bed of a nearly dry creek. Near that bridge, flames lapped at the timbers under the tracks.

"No panic now!" the conductor called as he hurried through the car. "Women, keep your children with you. Men and boys—all able-bodied people—we need your help!"

Already the smell of smoke drifted in through the windows. The moment the doors opened, men hurried down the steps. Libby grabbed her denim skirt from her bag and followed Peter off the train.

Pulling off their suit coats and shirts as they ran, men headed for the creek. Buckets in their hands, trainmen raced down the banks. Within moments a line formed.

Libby followed the others to the water. Already Peter had taken a place in the line. Standing in the creek, a man filled buckets. From one person to the next the buckets passed until the closest man emptied water on the flames.

As the empty buckets passed back along the line, there came a rhythm. Buckets filled, passed, emptied. Water sloshed against the burning railroad ties. Buckets returned to the creek.

Joining the women without children, Libby plunged her heavy skirt into the creek and ran up the bank. On the right side of the engine, the area of charred grass was growing larger. Leaping before the wind, the fire raced across the top of the tall grass, moving out across the prairie. But tongues of flame also crept along the tracks, as though trying to reach for the train.

Spreading out along that line, women pounded their shawls

or whatever clothing they could use against the burning grass. "Here! Over here!" a woman shouted.

Her long hair blowing in her face, Libby joined the line. Pounding her wet skirt against the flames, she felt the heat. Her throat burned with the smoke. Then she choked and had to pull back.

From behind her came the calls of men working together. "Faster! Faster!" someone cried. "The bridge! The fire's going toward the bridge!" called another.

Around Libby, the women worked steadily on. Now and then a hole opened in the line as a woman ran back to plunge a garment into the creek. Gradually the women started to gain on the fire.

Peter! Libby wondered once. *Where is he?*

Filled with panic, she whirled around, then saw him farther along the line, passing buckets to the men near the tracks. Libby drew a deep breath, glad to clear her lungs of the heavy smoke. At least the women were winning.

But when Libby raced to the creek, only small pools of water remained. Ahead of her, a bucket came up half full. Another was only a quarter full. Then, from high on top of the tender, Libby heard a cry.

"Up here! Toss me a bucket!"

Jordan knelt on the tender, the huge water tank behind the engine. Already he had thrown back the heavy cover.

"A rope!" he shouted, and someone threw one up.

Quickly Jordan knotted it around the handle of a bucket, then lowered the pail into the tender. When it came up full, the bucket line reformed. Swinging his pail over the side of the tank, Jordan lowered it to the ground. There a man emptied the water into another pail and sent the bucket down the line.

Again and again Jordan lowered his bucket into the tank of water, pulled it up, and lowered it to the men on the ground. Fanned by the wind, flames leaped along the wooden ties close to the bridge. At the head of the line, next to the trestle, Jordan's father poured water on the flames.

Libby plunged her denim skirt into the last bit of creek water, pulled it out dripping, and ran back to the line of women. The wind had shifted now, and the fire that had been moving away turned back. In a great arc it was circling around toward the end of the train.

Libby panicked. *Fire ahead of us. Fire behind? We'll be surrounded!*

Eating new grass as it came, the flames leaped across the prairie. As the line of women changed its position, Libby again pounded her skirt against the ground. Her arms ached now, and smoke rose around her, fueling her fear. *Can I possibly hold back my part of the line?*

Filled with terror, she glanced back toward the train. Two men stood behind the last car. At first Libby thought she was seeing things. Two men doing nothing while everyone else worked to put out a fire?

When the smoke lifted, one of the men was gone, but Libby recognized the other. *Riggs! Riggs standing there, while all around him people poured out their lives?*

For an instant Libby stared at him. Then the line of fire in front of her flared up again. Desperate now, Libby worked on.

Just as she felt she could do no more, Peter stood next to her. Skinny but strong, he pounded his wet shirt against the ground. Libby felt better just seeing him there. Side by side they worked until the ground around them was cinder black. The last flame was out.

In that moment a great shout went up. On the railroad ties closest to the bridge, men raised their arms in victory. Dragging whatever they had used to beat out the fire, exhausted women stumbled toward the engine.

All around her Libby saw their sweaty, soot-blackened faces. Their torn and dirty clothes. Their blistered hands, their hair blowing loose in the wind.

The shirtless men were as dirty and tired as the women. Like the women, some had singed hair and eyebrows. Others had welts on their faces and blistered skin.

Then, as if each person thought of the same thing in the same moment, they turned. As one person, they looked to the top of the tender where Jordan still knelt, a bucket of water in his hands.

When he dropped to the ground, men clapped his shoulders. Others shook his hand. Women offered their thanks. But Libby looked around. At the edge of the crowd stood Riggs, watching Jordan.

18

Mr. Lincoln's Springfield

Grabbing Peter's arm, Libby stepped out of sight behind the engine. Quickly she signed a *J* for Jordan, then an *R* for Riggs.

Peter nodded that he understood.

When they tried to warn Jordan, he had already slipped away. Libby could only wonder how the slavetrader had managed to board this train. Frances had been so careful to protect Jordan. Libby knew he was the last person on board. Riggs couldn't have followed him. *Unless—*

Libby's thoughts tumbled on. Like the ringing of a bell, she remembered the slavetrader's words to Micah: *"I came for your boy and found* you!"

While trainmen checked to see that the tracks and trestle were safe to use, one of the passengers filled the buckets with water. People began washing off their sweat and dirt. When Libby sloshed the clean water over her face and arms, she felt a welcome coolness after the heat of the fire.

As Peter finished washing, he pulled on his shirt and looked around. Glancing the same direction, Libby saw Jordan's father climbing into the baggage car. Again he walked hunched over like an old man, but during the fire he had forgotten his helpless look. As a strong, well-conditioned man, he had taken the difficult place next to the bridge. Libby had no doubt that Riggs had also seen Micah Parker.

Her throat tightened just thinking about Jordan's father. Hours before the rest of them boarded the train for Springfield, he had left Dr. Brown's house. The Underground Railroad conductor who helped Micah had driven a long distance to put him on this train. If it weren't for the fire, both Jordan and Micah would have been safe in the baggage car.

When the engineer blew a whistle for departure, Libby and Peter followed the rest of the passengers onto the train. As they returned to their seats, Libby saw that Peter's blond hair was singed near his forehead. Otherwise he seemed okay.

Taking the slate, Libby wrote to him. "After fighting a fire together, you seem like a brother."

Peter grinned with agreement, but then asked, "What do we do about Riggs?"

The dread within her growing, Libby turned her palms up and shrugged. She didn't know.

We need you, Caleb! she wanted to cry out. They also needed Allan Pinkerton's help.

As bad as the fire was, seeing Riggs upset Libby more. Right in this moment, here on this train, he might be collecting slave catchers to help him. Like a lion stalking its prey, Riggs would pounce on Jordan and Micah Parker the first chance he got.

There's only one way to solve the problem, Libby thought. *Somehow, some way, Jordan and his father need to get off the train before Riggs.*

Then, like a nightmare that still seemed real after she woke up, Libby remembered that two men had stood in back of the train. Riggs was one of them. Who was the other? The smoke had been too thick, her terror too great to be sure. Was he a friend or an enemy?

Any person who will not help to put out a fire has to be an enemy,

Libby decided. Worse still, whoever that man was, he, too, was on the train.

As Libby heard the *chug, chug, chug* of the train starting to roll again, she remembered something else—just dimly, not well enough to be sure. Were there two carpetbags on the ground next to the second man? If so, Libby knew who he was. *But I have to be sure!*

Still in her seat, Libby twisted around to see everyone sitting behind her. Then, looking toward the front, she let her gaze move from one person to the next. Seeing no one she knew, Libby wondered if she should walk through the other cars.

There was danger in that too. *If Riggs sees me, will he know I'm Captain Norstad's daughter and Jordan's friend?*

Thinking back, Libby tried to remember the times she had seen the cruel slavetrader. As far as she knew, Riggs had seen her with Jordan only one time—that spring night soon after she came to live on Pa's boat. Would Riggs remember her?

Finally Libby made up her mind. *I have to take the risk. I need to know who tipped off Riggs.*

Quickly Libby put on her bonnet so her red hair wouldn't be so noticeable. She tucked in the wisps curling around her face. Then she pushed the long strands inside the back of her dress and pulled up the collar.

"Be right back," she wrote to Peter, then stepped into the aisle.

The train was moving faster now, perhaps even thirty miles an hour. Libby felt the rumble of the wheels beneath her feet. Holding her breath, she walked forward into the next car. When she recognized no one there, she kept on through that car into the next.

Finally she spotted Riggs. She made her way slowly up the aisle, but just as she reached him, the car swayed. Libby wobbled, almost losing her balance, then grabbed the back of the seat in front of the slavetrader.

Hardly daring to breathe, Libby waited till the car steadied again. Then, trying to pretend that nothing had happened, she moved on.

In the car beyond that, Libby walked slowly enough to glance at every face. Partway up the aisle, Libby noticed the back of a man's head. Something about the way he sat seemed familiar. Then Libby noticed the color of his suit and his expensive-looking hat. Yes, that was the memory Libby held from the fire.

The swindler, Edward Dexter!

Turning quickly so he wouldn't see her, Libby started back through the cars. *So. How did Dexter get on the train without our seeing him?*

Then Libby realized it would have been easy. The swindler could have been part of the large group that boarded at Brighton. The conductor had sent some people forward, others back into different cars.

Dexter. The man who stole money from Pa. The man who stole money from Jordan. And now the man who is the link to Riggs.

When Libby sat down again next to Peter, she thought back to the telegraph office in Alton. *The swindler sent a message to Riggs. Dexter must have seen Jordan leave the* Christina. *But what happened in Brighton?*

Libby thought about it. Did the swindler see Jordan hiding on a wagon that took baggage to the train? If Dexter looked down from the second floor of the inn, he could have seen Jordan huddled between the trunks. All the swindler had to do was tell Riggs to get on that train.

Taking out Peter's slate, Libby wrote, "Edward Dexter."

"Here? On this train?" Peter asked.

When Libby nodded, shadows leaped into Peter's eyes.

Every ten miles the train came to one of the towns spaced out across the prairie. Each time the train stopped, Riggs stepped down to the platform. He kept an eye on the doors of the baggage car until the train started up again.

With each stop Libby grew more nervous. Before long they would reach Springfield. Jordan and his father would be forced to leave the car in plain sight.

"Are you sure Jordan knows he's in danger?" Peter asked.

"I'm sure," Libby wrote on the slate. "He must have seen Riggs during the fire."

But what if Jordan didn't? Just the idea that he might not know about the slavetrader overwhelmed Libby.

In that moment she heard the squeal of brakes. As the train clanked to a stop, Libby's heart leaped. *Another fire?* Here, too, the tall prairie grass looked tinder dry.

This time people peered from windows on both sides of the train. When Libby leaned out, she saw nothing unusual ahead of them. Looking back, she realized they had just crossed a small trestle that bridged the dry bed of a stream.

In that instant Libby caught a movement—Jordan jumping down from the baggage car. Running close to the stopped train, he slipped behind the last car. Moments later, he rolled down the bank and disappeared from view under the bridge.

Filled with relief, Libby breathed deep. Whatever had caused the train to stop had given Jordan just enough time. Now, if they could only go on before Riggs realized that Jordan was gone.

"Did you see that?" Peter whispered. "Jordan got away!"

Soon the conductor walked through the car. "We struck a cow wandering across the track. The cowcatcher protected the engine from damage. We'll have the tracks cleared in another minute."

Nervously twisting the cloth of her skirt, Libby waited. At last she felt the lurch of the train as it began to move. *Chugga, chugga, chugga,* faster and faster, the train went. When Libby finally leaned back, Peter whispered, "Jordan's daddy?"

"He'll leave soon," Libby wrote, believing Micah Parker would wait to see his son off the train.

At the next town, Libby looked back the moment the train stopped. To her dismay Riggs again stepped down to the platform. As he watched, then boarded the train again, Libby knew there were only a few more towns until Springfield. When was Micah going to make his move?

Again Libby watched at the next village. Again she did not see Micah jump out, but Riggs stepped down on the platform.

After a moment, he started toward the baggage car, as though to check whether Jordan and his father still rode on the train.

Suddenly Micah Parker leaped to the ground. As if wanting to be sure that Riggs saw him, Micah ran across the platform in full view of every onlooker.

"Stop!" Riggs cried out.

Instead, Micah raced toward the side of the station.

"Stop!" Riggs shouted. "Runaway slave!"

The man shifting baggage from the wagon to the train turned to look. A passenger wearing a tall hat watched Micah flee. Women quietly pulled their children closer to themselves.

When no one moved to help him, Riggs broke into a run. It was so unlike the man that it surprised Libby. Throwing aside all his usual dignity, he raced after Jordan's father. As Micah Parker disappeared around the corner of the station, Riggs was gaining on him.

Moments later the baggage handler finished unloading his cart. The engineer gave a warning whistle.

"Riggs will come back to the train," Libby wrote to Peter.

But Riggs didn't. Instead, the train pulled out of the station without him.

Libby and Peter watched through the window until the town disappeared from view. One moment Libby believed with all her heart that Jordan's daddy had gotten away. The next moment she felt deeply afraid.

"What if Micah Parker stumbled and fell?" she wrote to Peter. "What if men who want reward money heard Riggs shout?" Again Micah had protected his son—this time by jumping out before Riggs discovered that Jordan was gone.

The rest of the way to Springfield Libby thought about it. With each *clickety-clack* of the wheels she wondered, *Did Jordan's father get away? Or has he been captured again?*

When the train pulled into the Springfield station, Libby peered out the window until she saw the swindler climb down. Then she and Peter stepped into the aisle.

A woman carrying a large basket was in front of them, walking slowly toward the exit. Libby followed close behind, at the same time trying to keep a watch out the window. When Edward Dexter headed for a line of buggies, Libby felt sure he was going to hire one of them.

"Please, may we go past you?" Libby asked the woman who still blocked the aisle.

By the time Libby and Peter reached the steps, the swindler had climbed into a hack—a hired buggy with two horses. As the driver lifted the reins, Libby took a good look at him. She and Peter raced toward the last remaining hack, but a businessman reached the driver before them.

Filled with disappointment, Libby dropped down on a bench next to Peter. When the ten-year-old pushed his blond hair out of his eyes, it reminded her of Caleb. *Where are you, Caleb?* she wondered. *How long will it take you to travel to Brighton, then north again to Springfield?*

However long it took, she and Peter couldn't wait. It was up to them to find the swindler before he disappeared completely. *Before he hides the money, never to be found again!*

Libby didn't know where the thought came from, but she felt sure about one thing. The swindler wasn't going to carry the money forever. Somehow, somewhere, he would put it in a safe place—a place where he could return and get the money when he wanted.

Libby took Peter's slate. "How can we find the swindler?"

"The way Riggs found us," Peter answered.

Libby stared at him, then wrote. "Why didn't I think of that?"

In Alton Riggs saw us take the stage. When the driver came back, he asked questions. Knowing we went as far as the school for girls, it wouldn't be hard for Riggs to make the leap to Brighton. The village was a well-known haven for slaves.

Suddenly Libby knew what to do. "We'll wait around," she wrote to Peter. "We'll stay right here until that hack driver comes back."

Libby wasn't surprised when Peter simply nodded, as though he had already figured that out.

The time passed slowly, but at last passengers, freight, and hack drivers began arriving for the next train. Among the drivers was the one the swindler had hired.

"We need to find Mr. Dexter," Libby told him. "We saw him leave with you but couldn't catch you in time. Can you take us to where he went?"

"It's quite a ways," the driver answered. "Do you have enough money?"

Libby's heart sank. She had very little left after what she had given toward the stagecoach ride. But when she took out what she had, Peter offered his own coins.

"It's enough," the driver said. "Climb in."

After driving for a time, the hack driver entered a cemetery. As the horses followed a road along the top of a hill, the driver told them, "It was somewhere around here."

From here the hill dropped away in different directions. Between the steep hills, narrow valleys, or ravines, lay like creases in the land. Here and there were gravestones.

But the driver was still looking around. "This doesn't seem quite right," he said. Calling "Giddyup!" to the horses, he drove on.

Before long the driver stopped again, this time next to a smoothed-out patch of dirt not far from the road. "Maybe this is the place," he said.

"We need a shovel," Peter whispered to Libby.

Spotting nearby trees and bushes, Libby marked the place in her mind. "Did Mr. Dexter get out here?" she asked. When the driver shook his head, Libby asked if he knew where Mr. Dexter stayed while in town.

"He had me leave him off near the square."

Where he could take another hack, Libby thought. *Or walk in any direction.*

"Do you want me to take you somewhere?" the driver asked.

Remembering how they had been followed before, Libby knew better than to ask for the Colored Baptist Church. "We'd like to see the State of Illinois Capitol Building," she said.

The next time the driver stopped, it was before a large, beautiful building built with rose-colored stone. Four tall pillars supported the roof over the entry. Above that, centered on the larger roof, were more pillars and a great dome. The building looked strong and sure, something Libby needed in her life right now. Seeing it, she felt better.

When they found no hack drivers at the square, Libby took the slate and wrote quickly to Peter. "Why do you think the swindler went to the cemetery?"

"To bury the money," Peter answered.

"In broad daylight?"

"If no one was around."

Libby remembered the patches of dirt. Though the driver was uncertain about which patch, he had been sure of one thing. The swindler had been interested in places where the ground had been dug up.

"If we need a shovel, so does Dexter," Libby wrote. "And something to bury the money in."

"He probably bought a chest and went back with a different hack driver," Peter said.

By now both Libby and Peter were so hungry they felt they hadn't eaten in weeks. Looking around, they found a bench outside a barber shop. As they finished the sandwiches Frances had given them, a tall thin man with dark brown hair and a stovepipe hat came out.

Suddenly he stopped right in front of Libby and Peter. Taking off his hat, he flipped through the papers he carried inside. Then, looking as if he had what he needed, the man walked on again.

It made Libby curious. "How come that man carries papers in his hat?" she asked the barber who came outside.

"Why, that's Mr. Lincoln," he said. "Abraham Lincoln. When he was a young postmaster in New Salem, he carried letters that way. Kept them safe, he figured. Now that he's a lawyer, he carries important papers the same way."

As Libby watched, Mr. Lincoln crossed the street to the Capitol building. "Do you know him?" she asked.

"Yes'm. I'm Billy Florville. Mr. Lincoln is my friend."

"Can you tell me something else?" Libby asked. "We need to find the Colored Baptist Church in Springfield."

"The members meet in a house," Billy said. "You might find someone home right now."

When the barber gave directions, Libby and Peter discovered they didn't have far to go. As they drew close to the house, Peter looked down the street. Excitement in his face, he cried, "It's Jordan!"

19

Trick Or . . . ?

When Jordan saw Libby and Peter, he broke into a run. "My daddy?" he asked the moment they met. "What happened to him?"

"He left the train two stops after you," Libby said. "He waited as if he wanted to make sure Riggs saw him. Then he raced across the platform. Riggs followed him."

"Did Daddy get away?"

In the hours since Libby's last sight of Micah Parker, she had kept hoping that he escaped. She wanted to pass that hope along to Jordan. Yet Libby knew she had to be honest.

"The last I saw him, your daddy was ahead." Libby tried to push away her next thought. *And Riggs was running fast.*

After rolling down the bank next to the railroad tracks, Jordan had hid under the bridge, then walked to the nearest town. There he used his pass to climb aboard the next train for Springfield. When Libby told him about the swindler, Jordan's eyes lit up.

"Let's get a shovel and see what we can find."

When they knocked on the door of the home used as a meeting place for the Colored Baptist Church, the woman who lived there welcomed them in. Jordan poured out his story.

"We'll be on the lookout for your daddy," the woman promised him. "Now, what do you need? A shovel? Some food? A lantern? It'll be dark soon."

Libby smiled. It felt good to have someone watching out for them.

When she and Jordan and Peter were ready to leave, the woman told them, "If you need a place to stay tonight, just come on back."

As they walked the few miles to the cemetery, the sun dropped lower and lower in the sky. By the time they got there, the trees and tombstones cast long shadows across the ground.

Peter took one look at the spot the hack driver showed them and said, "This isn't the right place."

"Why?" Libby wrote on the slate.

"The swindler would be afraid to be inside a cemetery."

"Afraid?" The idea seemed strange to Libby. "A cemetery should be special for people who have loved ones buried there."

Then she remembered. Girls in her Chicago school thought that ghosts haunted cemeteries. Libby felt sure the girls were wrong.

"Let's look around," Jordan said. Already he had been doing just that—looking over his shoulder often, as if he expected Riggs or Dexter to be lurking behind a tree.

But Peter led them outside the cemetery. Before long, they found just what they were looking for—a small square of ground that had been dug up.

As the sky turned orange and red in the west, Jordan began digging. Before long, the shovel clinked against metal.

"That's it!" Jordan cried. "A good, hard box with lots of money!"

Soon Jordan had all the dirt off the top. He and Peter pulled up a small black chest.

Jordan's face glowed with excitement. The worry he had felt about the stolen money seemed to slide off his back.

Libby's excitement bubbled up. "Your name will be cleared," she told Jordan. "And Pa can make the payment on the *Christina*!"

When Jordan shook the chest, it made no noise. "Lots of paper money in here!" he said. Then he turned it over to open it, and his excitement changed to disappointment. "It's locked!"

"Then it's the swindler's treasure for sure!" Libby exclaimed. "Why else would a locked chest be buried here?"

Even so, she felt an uneasy nudge. *What if I'm wrong? What if it really doesn't hold Pa's money and what Reverend Freeman calls the Lord's treasure?*

Afraid that someone might be watching them, Libby looked around. By now the orange light of the setting sun had started to fade. In the dusky grayness between sundown and night, every tree seemed to hide someone—a person standing straight and tall behind the trunk.

"We better leave the treasure here," Libby said.

"Leave it?" Clearly Jordan didn't like the idea.

"If we take it, we can't prove the swindler buried it," Libby answered. "If he comes back to dig it up, and we catch him in the act—"

"But if he comes back, and we ain't here to see him—"

Even the thought of such a possibility frightened Libby. In twelve days Pa had to make his payment on the *Christina.* Jordan needed to restore the faith his church had put in him. Fugitives in Chicago needed money for the boat ride to Canada. But as she felt the pressure of time, Libby remembered something else.

As if it were still happening, she remembered one scene after another: Pa standing on the deck of the *Christina,* telling Dexter he couldn't swindle an immigrant. Reverend Freeman saying, "Let's not accuse someone unjustly." Caleb and Jordan standing near Elijah Lovejoy's unmarked grave. Dr. Brown pleading with Riggs for the life of a slave. Micah Parker sacrificing his own freedom for his son. All those men—Pa, Reverend Freeman, Elijah Lovejoy, Dr. Brown, Micah Parker—had stood for something important.

And women, too—Priscilla Baltimore, rowing fugitives

across the wide Mississippi, making sure that slaves learned about Jesus. Frances Brown, hiding runaways, reading Bible stories to them in the attic.

Libby drew a deep breath. What she and Jordan and Peter needed to do seemed simple in comparison with all that. "If we don't stop the swindler, he'll keep on hurting people," Libby said.

When Libby explained to Peter, he agreed. Jordan thought about it a moment longer, then said, "We need to leave the money, all right. But planting it in the ground sure scares me."

Jordan's fear made Libby even more uneasy. More than once she had seen how well Jordan heard the Lord. More than once that still, small voice inside Jordan had helped them find their way. *Now that we've found the money, what if we lose it again?*

Then, as though Jordan guessed Libby's thoughts, he said, "But it ain't the Lord making me scared."

With each of them taking a handle, Jordan and Peter lowered the chest into the hole again. Peter shoveled the dirt into place. Jordan smoothed it out until the ground looked the way they found it.

From that moment on, the three of them kept watch on the place where the treasure was buried. Two at a time, they waited behind a large rock and some bushes, always afraid they would miss the swindler when he returned. Men from the Colored Baptist Church started taking turns, watching with them.

When Libby looked up the address Allan Pinkerton had given her, no one was there. That made Libby even more nervous. Pa wanted them to get help from a law officer if they needed it. Libby hoped that help could be Mr. Pinkerton. Then she discovered the house where he planned to stay belonged to a Springfield policeman, and she felt better.

As Monday night turned into Tuesday, Wednesday, Thursday, and then Friday, Libby grew more tired and more frantic. *What if we're watching a box that isn't really the treasure?*

But their troubles were much bigger than that. As one day followed the next, Jordan's daddy did not reach Springfield.

With each day Jordan seemed to grow thinner, his eyes darker with fear.

Added to that, Libby, Jordan, and Peter kept wondering what had happened to Caleb. *If all goes well, the ride from Brighton to Springfield takes about two hours,* Libby remembered. *How can a two-hour ride take all week?*

Ever since meeting Caleb, Libby had dreaded the idea of someone hurting him because of his work with the Underground Railroad. Now she wondered if her worst fears had come true.

Where are you, Caleb? Libby's heart cried out. *Are you safe? What has happened to you?*

Day after day, the family living at the house used by the Colored Baptist Church gave Libby, Jordan, and Peter a place to stay. Throughout the week the family fed and encouraged them. Yet on Saturday morning, Libby woke up feeling as if she couldn't handle another moment of waiting. *Exactly one week from today Pa needs that money. And we still need to find Pa and get to Galena.*

Climbing out of bed, she walked over to a window. Standing in the light, she began to pray. "Lord, I always depend on Caleb. I don't know what to do."

But I know. Like a still, small voice the words came. *Ask me.*

Instantly Libby prayed. "Lord, I do! I ask you to show me."

In the stillness Libby listened. From somewhere in the house, she heard the chiming of a clock. From down the street came the rumble of a wagon. Then from near at hand—as near as Libby's mind and spirit—she remembered Caleb's verse: *"The Lord is my light and my salvation; whom shall I fear? The Lord is the strength of my life; of whom shall I be afraid?"*

At last Libby knew what to pray. "Lord, right now, in this moment, I'm making a choice—to depend upon *you.*"

After supper that evening, Libby walked alone to meet Jordan and Peter near the swindler's treasure. By the time she reached the large rock, it was dark. To her dismay neither Jordan nor Peter was there.

Something happened, Libby thought. *Why did Peter leave? Why isn't Jordan here?*

Her first thought was that the swindler had come for the treasure, and the boys followed him. But the ground wasn't dug up.

"Where are you, Jordan?" she wanted to cry out. "Where are you, Peter? Why aren't you here?" Turning every direction, Libby tried to find some hint of where they could be.

Fearful now, she began praying again. There could be only one reason for both of them being gone. Something was wrong.

Then, as Libby prayed, a memory flashed into her mind. Riggs standing at the back of the train during the prairie fire. Riggs talking to the swindler while everyone else worked desperately to put out the fire.

In that moment Libby remembered something she had seen but hadn't thought about. *Riggs gave money to the swindler. Why?*

Either the swindler had already done something for Riggs or the swindler was about to do something for him.

Like a thunderbolt, a thought entered Libby's mind. *Has Edward Dexter somehow tricked Jordan about his father?*

Just thinking about such a terrible thing filled Libby with panic. More than once Caleb had said, "The one place where Jordan doesn't use good judgment is when he gets scared about his family."

Feeling desperate, Libby started walking around. When she came to the top of a hill, darkness veiled the trees, the bushes, the narrow valleys between hills. With growing fear, she peered into the night, trying to see.

Then, as if someone were walking through a ravine, Libby saw the light of a lantern below her. The lantern moved from side to side, as if the person who held it could not walk a straight line. *Peter!*

Trying to keep the light in sight, Libby started after him. There could be only one reason for Peter leaving the treasure. He had to be following Jordan. That had to mean Jordan needed help.

But what if I'm wrong? Libby asked herself. *What if this is a trick to get us away from the treasure? What if the swindler comes while we're*

all gone? If he digs up the treasure and disappears, Pa loses the Christina*!*

Still staring at the light, Libby stopped. *How can I make such a choice? I'm walking away from helping my own father! From saving the* Christina*—Pa's hiding place for fugitives, Pa's way to earn a living, our home!*

20

Nobody Knows

Torn by fear, Libby stood there. Then she remembered Pa standing up to the swindler in spite of great cost. She remembered Micah Parker giving himself away so his son could escape.

Libby drew a deep breath. *What is money—even our boat—compared to Jordan's freedom and perhaps his life?*

The light was gone now, but when Libby started walking, she saw it again. Faster and faster Libby hurried in the darkness, trying to catch up. Then Peter passed onto a road. Sometimes he was harder to see, but still the light bobbed back and forth.

As the ground leveled out, Libby started to run. Staying on the grass, she tried to move without sound. Then she realized Peter was passing close to the house where Allan Pinkerton said he would be. *Can I find Mr. Pinkerton and not lose Peter?*

By the time Libby reached the house, she was out of breath. The moment she pounded on the door, Mr. Pinkerton answered.

"Come!" Libby cried. "We need help!"

For one moment Mr. Pinkerton stepped back into the house.

When he returned, a man in a policeman's uniform followed him.

Once more Libby broke into a run. A block farther on, she saw Peter again. A block beyond that, he started to slow down. As Libby drew close to Peter, she understood why. A short distance ahead of him, a man carried a lantern—a man whose broad back looked like that of the swindler. With him walked a boy who seemed to be Jordan.

When the boy started to follow the man up the steps of a house, Libby cried out, "Jordan!"

Instantly Mr. Pinkerton and the policeman stepped behind a large pine tree. As the swindler turned, his gaze took in Peter and Libby.

"What are you doing here?" Dexter demanded.

"Jordan!" Libby called again. "Don't believe what he's telling you!"

With her words Jordan moved away from the swindler. When Dexter tried to grab his arm, Jordan leaped out of reach and hurried over to Libby and Peter.

For one instant the swindler stared at all of them. As if knowing he was outnumbered, his eyes filled with hate. "Go! All of you!"

Without another word he opened the front door, stepped into the house, and slammed the door behind him.

"He said my daddy got hurt running away," Jordan told Libby and Peter. "He said he'd take me to him. It's not true? My daddy ain't here?"

"I don't think so," Libby said. "I think it was Dexter's way to get you to follow him. Is that why you went with him?"

"I thought maybe he was lying." Jordan's shoulders slumped with discouragement. He kicked a stone on the street, then looked up. "You think the swindler wants the reward on my head?"

In that instant Libby realized something. "Dexter gave up too easily!"

As Jordan stared at her, Libby's thoughts tumbled on. *Does that mean Dexter doesn't have slave catchers to help? Or is he trading the hope of Jordan's reward for the bigger treasure he buried? If Jordan kicked up a fuss, the swindler wouldn't be able to leave town with his treasure.*

Suddenly Libby broke into a run. Slipping from tree to tree, she moved close to the house and crouched down. As she crept along the side wall, she heard the back door open, then close. Moments later she saw the dark hulk of a body pass through the yard toward a garden gate. When the gate squeaked, Libby caught the glint of moonlight upon metal. Did the swindler carry a shovel?

Turning, Libby saw with relief that Peter was right behind her. *So! Once again he guessed what the swindler was doing!*

Behind Peter were Jordan, Mr. Pinkerton, and the policeman. By the time Libby followed Dexter through the yard and the gate, he was already out of sight. Libby gulped with panic. She had all she could do not to race ahead until she once again saw the swindler. Then she remembered. *I don't need to see him. I know where he's going.*

When Dexter started climbing a hill, his dark shape moved into sight for a minute or two. Then he once again disappeared.

Libby and the others walked faster now. Peter's lantern was no longer lit. In the darkness he reached out and took Libby's elbow. Just knowing he was there made her feel better.

Passing through the ravines, all of them moved swiftly but without sound. By the time they reached the large rock near the hiding place, Libby heard the clink of metal against metal. Hiding behind thick bushes, she and the others knelt down and watched.

Soon Dexter finished shoveling earth from the hole. Down on his knees he lifted the small chest. Setting it aside, he shoveled dirt back into the hole and smoothed it out. Then he hid the shovel beneath some bushes.

When Dexter went back to pick up the chest, Peter moved out from where he hid.

"You again!" The man glared at Peter. "What are you doing here?"

For an instant Peter shrank back. Yet Libby knew he had not heard the swindler's words. Instead, the angry expression on Dexter's face made it clear what he was saying.

Shaking a fist, Dexter started toward Peter. Just then Allan Pinkerton and the policeman stepped out. Looking at Peter, the detective motioned toward Dexter. Lifting his shoulders as if in a question, Mr. Pinkerton seemed to ask, "You know this man? How?"

"From Galena," Peter answered. "I lived at his house."

Libby stared at Peter. "You *lived* at his house? That's how you know him?"

But Peter was watching the swindler. As though to help Mr. Pinkerton ask questions, he pulled out his slate. Strong now, even in the way he stood, Peter looked directly at Dexter. "You were trying to turn me into a thief like you."

Suddenly Dexter rushed forward. Before anyone could stop him, he grabbed Peter's slate and slung it away. As it crashed against the trunk of a tree, the slate shattered into many tiny pieces.

As Dexter hurried back to the treasure, Mr. Pinkerton commanded, "Stop!" With a few quick steps, he caught up to Dexter and grabbed his arms. The policeman snapped handcuffs around the swindler's wrists.

Jordan took one handle of the chest and Peter the other. Hardly daring to hope that their search for the stolen money had ended, Libby walked with the boys and Mr. Pinkerton and his friend to the police station. When Dexter was searched, the policeman found a small key that fit the chest.

With Edward Dexter in a cell and the policeman standing nearby, Mr. Pinkerton spoke to Libby and Jordan. "Now, tell me again what you think might be in this chest."

When Libby told him the amount of money stolen from Pa, Jordan gave the amount from his church. "Reverend Freeman told me there are ink blotches on about ten of the bills."

Picking up the key, Mr. Pinkerton handed it to Jordan. His hand shook with excitement as he turned the key in the lock and opened the chest. Inside were two separate bags filled with money.

When the policeman finished counting the money in the first bag, it came to the exact amount Libby had told him. When he finished with the second bag, he winked at Jordan. "To the dollar," he said.

Jordan spread out the bills on the table. On some of the corners were ink blotches.

With Peter's slate broken, Libby snatched up a piece of paper and a pen from a nearby desk. Quickly she wrote to Peter, "The swindler was the man you stayed with?"

"Until last summer I lived with a family in Galena when I came home from school. But they moved away, and the swindler offered to take care of me. When he stole something and thought he might get caught, he had me carry the carpetbag with the stolen money."

Again Libby wrote, "Dexter's note to Pa said, 'Tell Peter to remember what I taught him.' What did Dexter teach you?"

Peter flushed with embarrassment. "He tried to teach me to steal any way I could."

Libby stared at him, then wrote as fast as she could. "So he sent you on the *Christina*? He expected you to steal from Pa or anyone else?"

Peter smiled, that strange smile that always warmed Libby's heart. "But I didn't steal from anyone."

In that moment Libby remembered Pa's words. *He wanted Peter to grow up living in the sunlight.*

All of the pieces had fallen into place. All of the pieces except what had happened to Caleb and to Jordan's father. And those pieces were the most important of all.

Leaving the money at the police station, Libby, Jordan, and Peter went outside. Far above them, bright stars twinkled against the night sky.

As they walked to the house where they had been staying, the darkness of night turned to the gray light before dawn. One by one the stars disappeared. But one star remained, brighter than any other. Was it the Morning Star?

Drawing close to the house, Libby looked ahead. When she saw someone with Caleb's blond hair coming along the road, she wondered if she was imagining things. *Is it him? Can it be?*

As Libby started running, Jordan and Peter ran with her. When they reached Caleb, he threw his arms around all three of them at once. Then all of them were laughing with relief, silly with finding each other again.

"Whatever happened to you?" Libby asked. In all the time she had known him, Caleb never looked better. "We've been worried all week."

When they started toward the house, Caleb explained. "By the time I got the horses to Dr. Brown's barn, it was too late to leave. Slave catchers had found the marks in the riverbank. They were swarming all over, wanting the rewards for Jordan and Micah Parker."

"The catchers saw you?" It was what Libby dreaded.

Caleb nodded. "They couldn't prove anything. Jordan and his father were gone. But if I had come straight here, I would have led them to Jordan and his father."

Caleb faced his friend. "Where is he? Your daddy isn't here yet?"

When Jordan shook his head, the glad light of seeing Caleb disappeared from his eyes.

Three Sundays, Libby thought later that morning as she and Caleb, Jordan, and Peter sat down in church. After breakfast, Libby had helped the woman of the house arrange the chairs in rows.

Three Sundays, and each of them so different. The first in Galena when Jordan learned the money had been stolen. The second at the Presbyterian church next to the school for girls. And now another week had passed. Of all the weeks in Jordan's life, perhaps this had been the longest. Three times he had found his father. Three times he had lost his daddy again.

As Libby saw the pain in Jordan's eyes, she guessed what he was thinking. How could it take seven days to travel the short distance from where Micah left the train to Springfield? Something had to be terribly wrong.

Though they had found the money for Pa and for Jordan's church, Libby felt no joy. Compared to Micah's life, the money didn't matter at all.

With a borrowed slate in her hand, Libby sat next to Peter, writing as needed. When the people started singing the closing hymn, Jordan stood up and stumbled forward. As though unable to carry his worries anymore, he dropped to his knees and began to pray.

"Oh, Lord! Precious Jesus! Where can my daddy be? We don't know if he is dead or alive. Please, Lord. Bring my daddy to us!"

Suddenly Jordan's strong shoulders heaved. His entire body trembled as he broke down weeping.

Quietly Caleb stood up. Dropping down on Jordan's left side, Caleb put his arm around the shoulders of his friend. When Caleb bowed his head, Libby knew he was praying.

Without making a sound, she, too, stood up. Hardly knowing how she got there, Libby knelt down on the floor next to her chair. With her whole heart she prayed as she had seldom prayed before.

Dimly she became aware of what was happening around her. Peter kneeling on the floor next to her. Then members of the church leaving their chairs. One by one they knelt down behind Jordan or wherever they found room.

At first the people prayed silently, as Libby had. Then from here or there, Libby heard a whisper. "Precious Jesus! Blessed Savior!"

Before long the whisper grew, with people praying aloud all at once. "Good Lord! Precious Savior! Alleluia, Jesus!" Like a choir of voices that spoke instead of singing, the sound grew bold and strong, pleading before the throne of God. Then, as gradually as the prayers built up, the voices grew quiet.

"Thank you, Lord," Jordan whispered. "Thank you, Jesus."

Softly, in no more than a whisper, others echoed his prayer.

Deep and low, someone began to sing:

Nobody knows the trouble I see,
Nobody knows but Jesus;
Nobody knows the trouble I see,
Glory, Hallelujah!

As though filled with peace, Jordan drew a deep breath. Yet still he knelt there, as if waiting.

Sometimes I'm up, sometimes I'm down,
O yes, Lord!
Sometimes I'm almost to the ground—

From the back of the room, Libby heard a creak in the floor. A moment later she heard the shuffle of a bare foot passing near her chair. Looking up, Libby saw a tall man kneel down on the floor next to Jordan. Reaching out, the man laid his arm on top of Caleb's where it stretched around Jordan's shoulders.

"I is here, Jordan," his daddy said quietly.

Jordan's head shot up. "Daddy!" As though unable to believe what he saw, Jordan stared at him. "Just when I found you, I lost you again. I didn't know where you were!"

"I hid in the cistern next to the tracks."

"In the water?"

"It weren't enough to drown a man like me. When it was safe to climb out, I used the bucket and rope. The man who handled the baggage hid me till I walked here to find you."

Suddenly Jordan began to weep all over again. The harder he sobbed, the more his father's arm tightened around him. Around them the singing grew stronger.

Nobody knows the trouble I see,
Nobody knows but Jesus—

Now a shout of joy filled the words. *Glory, Hallelujah!*

At last Jordan looked up into his daddy's eyes. "You are really free!"

Micah Parker's voice was husky, as if he, too, had been weeping. "I is free to be with you. To be with your momma and Serena and Zack and little Rose."

Only then did Libby remember. *It's Jordan's birthday! The day when he knows his daddy is free!*

As people started to leave for home, Libby, Caleb, and Peter went outside. In the morning sunlight, they sat down on the grass to talk about what had happened.

Using the slate, Libby explained to Peter, "When Micah Parker walks in the door, Jordan's mother isn't going to believe what she's seeing!"

Since the spring day when Jordan first came on the boat, there had been something Libby knew. Though separated by slavery, Jordan belonged to a never-give-up family—a family that cared for each other no matter how difficult things were.

Just imagining their reunion, Libby felt as though she wanted to shout with gladness.

Caleb's grin told her he felt the same way. Yet he had a warning. "Somehow all of Jordan's family still has to get together."

Not wanting to think about the danger that might lie ahead, Libby pushed Caleb's words aside. Instead she glanced toward Peter. The look in his eyes told Libby that he understood exactly what had happened. Perhaps he understood even better than the rest of them.

Now Peter spoke softly. "I have a family too."

Taking the slate, Libby began writing again. As tears welled up in her eyes, the words blurred. She didn't want to erase them, but to keep them on the slate forever.

When she finished, she held out the words to Peter. "I'm glad I have a new brother."

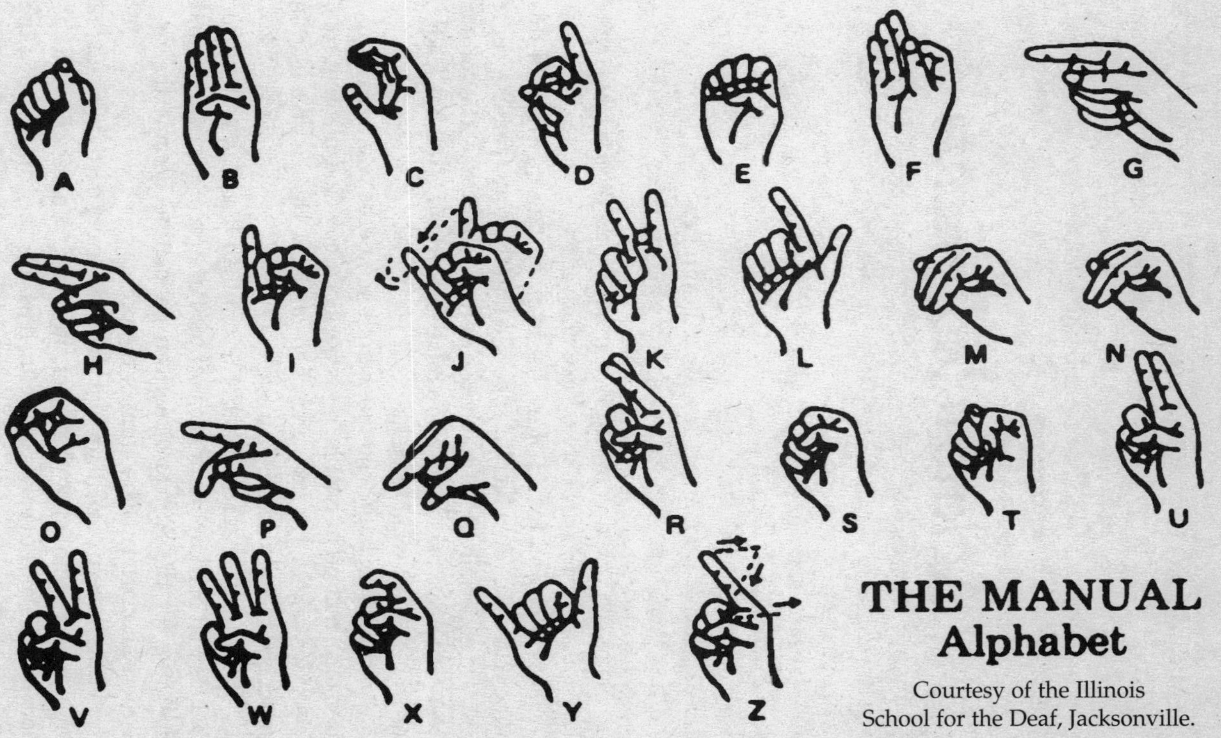

THE MANUAL
Alphabet

Courtesy of the Illinois
School for the Deaf, Jacksonville.

Acknowledgments

Have you asked yourself, *Who are my heroes? Who are the people I believe in and trust and want to shape my life after?*

For Caleb and for all of us, it's an important question. In this time when we often feel disappointed by the way famous people act, we especially want to choose heroes who are worthy of our respect. Such a person may be a relative or friend, a teacher, leader, or someone we want to be like.

In thinking about who our heroes should be, we need to understand that no human being is perfect. Only God fills that role. Yet if we ask for His help and choose wisely, He can give us role models who help us grow strong.

In life and in death, Caleb's hero, Elijah P. Lovejoy, stood for beliefs that are important to all of us. Because of his courage and his love for the African-American people, he became the first American martyr for freedom of the press.

With the help of William Johnson, a cemetery custodian and the only person who knew the exact site, Major Hunter changed the location of Mr. Lovejoy's grave in 1864. During a time when the principles of free speech and free press meant much to him, editor Thomas Dimmock placed a marker on the grave. Through his work and the cooperation of the people of Alton and the state of Illinois, a one-hundred-foot-high monument to Lovejoy was completed in 1897. 1997 marks the 100-year anniversary of this memorial dedicated "In Gratitude to God and in the Love of Liberty."

On every November 9 since 1864, those who wish to honor Elijah Lovejoy and the beliefs for which he stood have gathered for a memorial service. All are welcome to join them at noon at the Lovejoy Monument in Alton, Illinois.

In a letter to the African Americans of Alton, Mr. Dimmock asked them to protect and care for Mr. Lovejoy's grave. By tradition, the trustee of the grave site has always been an African American. Those chosen for this position regard it as a sacred honor. However, the president and other members of the Elijah P. Lovejoy Memorial Board of Directors have been both African American and white. When the association received its charter in 1952, it became the first nonreligious organization in Alton with an interracial leadership.

The association membership is made up of black and white citizens who want to live Mr. Lovejoy's call to defend the great constitutional principles of human rights and a free press. Mr. Lovejoy knew that the country would survive only as long as there were men and women who would defend those values with their lives.

As the Alton Historical Society reminds us, "The vigil in Alton has become the American vigil—a determination to maintain freedom and justice for all men and women. It is a vigil of peace, the longing for a day when we shall beat our swords into plowshares and spears into pruning hooks."

Alton AME Church is now called Campbell Chapel. In the early history of Illinois, this church was joined by three other AME churches—New Bethel-Rocky Fork, Allen Chapel, and Model Chapel. Priscilla Baltimore was Alton's own Harriet Tubman. Reverend John Livingston is believed to be the first pastor of Union Baptist Church in Alton. He also organized Mt. Emory Baptist Church in Jacksonville and what is now called the Zion Missionary Baptist Church in Springfield. Known for his missionary efforts in the region, Reverend Livingston has been called the father of the

Colored Baptists in Illinois. He lived to be an amazing 105 years old.

Monticello Seminary, the school for girls, is now the Lewis and Clark Community College. The nearby church has been moved across the road and is used as a chapel for weddings.

In Brighton some of the buildings used as Underground Railroad stops are still in use. Over the years houses have been built between the "stations," so that today the lantern signal would not be possible. Yes, Dr. Brown's loss of a fugitive and the magistrate's statement that he would not make an arrest on Sunday are true to history. Years later, Frances Brown loved to tell people how she read Bible stories to fugitives hiding in their home.

I am deeply grateful for all who have helped me in the writing of this book. Four people gave an enormous amount of time in providing information about the people and history of their cities. There is much I could say about the giftedness of J. Eric Robinson, for his strong sense of story helped me lay out the scenes in Alton. Yet when I attempted to describe his many accomplishments, he simply said, "I am Eric Robinson, president of the Elijah P. Lovejoy Memorial." Thanks, Eric! And my heartfelt gratitude to Charlene Gill, president, Alton Area Historical Society; and June Wilderman, president, Brighton Heritage Group and curator of the Brighton Museum. In addition to providing information, these people read portions of the manuscript. Many thanks also to Jessie Mae Finley, historian emeritus, of the Zion Missionary Baptist Church, Springfield.

H. Scott Wolfe, historical librarian of the Galena Public Library District, Galena, Illinois, also provided details and read part of the manuscript. Thanks to Susan Kulasekara, adult services librarian, Hayner Public Library District, Alton; Sister Wilma Wittman, Ursuline Convent, Alton; Kim Bauer, historical research specialist, and E. Cheryl Schnirring, curator of manuscripts at the Illinois State Historical Library; and William Tubbs, Associate Editor, *Illinois Historical Journal,* Springfield. J. Hurley and Roberta Hagood, authors of such classic books as *The Story of Hannibal* and *Hannibal, Too,* helped Libby celebrate her birthday.

A number of people have helped Peter come to life. You may

wonder about his explanation of how he became deaf. The term *brain fever* was often used in the years in which this book is set. Because of the historical time frame, we don't know exactly what was meant. We do know that many people lost their hearing or died from brain fever because it was highly contagious.

My life has been made rich by Tilly (Caroline) Raven and by the students, faculty, and staff of the Illinois School for the Deaf in Jacksonville. Kathleen Cook, second-grade teacher, and Marene Mattern, educator aide, have worked long hours to teach me, answer my questions, and then help with the manuscript. A million thanks, Kathy and Marene!

My gratitude also to Dude Wildrick, junior high principal; teachers Nancy Kelly-Jones and Joe Lee; and interpreter Christine Good. Thanks to Joan M. Forney, superintendent of the Illinois School for the Deaf, for permission to use the finger alphabet chart in this book.

Wanda Tiffany, curator, Heritage Cultural Center, introduced me to Kathy Cook and other new friends in Jacksonville: Jack Barwick, president, Jacksonville Historical Society; Art Wilson, freelance writer; and Dr. Jim Davis, history professor at Illinois College. And thanks to the librarians at Schewe Library, Illinois College, and the Jacksonville Public Library.

I'm grateful to Jessica Swanson, championship jumper and championship person, who knows horses much better than I do; and Tim Schandel, senior museum assistant, Lake Superior Museum of Transportation, Duluth, Minnesota.

Thanks to my in-house editors, Rochelle Glöege and Natasha Sperling, and the entire Bethany House team. Thanks to all of you readers and friends who have found a variety of ways to offer your encouragement and love.

Finally, my deep gratitude to my great husband, Roy, and my editor, Ron Klug. Both of you have profoundly influenced each one of the novels in this series. May the way you have blessed me be returned to you countless times over.